Beneath the Rainbow

LISA SHAMBROOK

LAST KRYSTALLOS
PUBLISHING

Cover photograph © 2012 Bekah Shambrook
Cover concept by Lisa Shambrook

Cover design by Lisa Shambrook and Blue Harvest Creative
Interior book design and eBook design by Blue Harvest Creative
www.blueharvestcreative.com

Beneath *the* Rainbow

Copyright © 2011, 2013 Lisa Shambrook

All rights reserved. Except as permitted under the U.S. Copyright Act of 1976, no part of this publication may be reproduced, distributed, or transmitted in any form or by any means, or stored in a database or retrieval system, without prior written permission of the publisher.

This book is a work of fiction. The characters, incidents, and dialogue are drawn from the author's imagination and are not to be construed as real. Any resemblance to actual events or persons, living or dead is entirely coincidental.

Published by
Last Krystallos Publishing

ISBN-13: 978-1492701057
ISBN-10: 149270105X

Visit the author at:
www.lisashambrook.com
www.thelastkrystallos.wordpress.com
www.facebook.com/pages/LisaShambrookAuthor
www.twitter.com/LastKrystallos

This book is for Bekah, Dan and Caitlin
and Vince
May we all reach that distant star...

ONE
SWING

Freya was seven-years-old when she got hit by the car. It was a 4x4 with a bull bar.

◆◆◆◆◆

Freya raced ahead, full of giggles and determination, keen to reach the swings before Mum changed her mind and yielded to Jasmine's drowsy grumbles. As the morning sun spilled its rays she ignored Mum's groan and her baby sister's whine, and sprinted ahead. Moments later she scrambled onto the swing, her smile as big as her anticipation.

Freya couldn't wait to swing as high as she could and feel the rush that made her stomach tumble...

So she swung, pumping her little legs to and fro, thrusting her body forward and back again as the swing gained momentum. She loved swinging, loved the wind rushing through her hair and caressing her bare arms.

Freya laughed as the swing planted a tickle in her stomach. She giggled and pumped harder. She closed her eyes and gripped the chains, pushing outward with as much force as her arms allowed.

As she swung her mind wandered. She opened her eyes and stared up at the sky. It was blue. It hadn't been blue, not blue like this, for a long time. This blue was deep, bright and strong like the blue in Dad's favourite t-shirt. This blue ruled the sky and banished clouds forever. Freya laughed, and the impetus of the swing tickled her tummy again, sending ripples of joy to her head.

Freya, free and flying, launched up into the pure, blue sky… Freya was a bird, flapping her wings and soaring, free from gravity, free from the irritating grizzles springing from the pushchair, free from her mother's sighs and best of all, free from restriction.

The chains went slack and the seat she was cradled in jumped as she reached its zenith. She was as high as she could go, but she kept it going, the seat jerking every time she hit her apex. Her hands gripping that tiny piece of freedom like it was the last thing she would ever do…

It was.

Who wants to listen to mother's restraining call when you're having so much fun? Who wants to go home holding onto a slow pushchair when you can fly, your little feet propelling you, and your imagination, along the tarmac with wings? She ran, charging through the open park gates. The huge, black railings, like prison bars, released her and the driver of the 4x4 had no chance to stop.

The skid marks, that decorated the road for many months after, did not begin until Freya's tiny body had been flung aside.

Screams echoed in Freya's head, nothing else, just screams, and her mother's screams pierced her through.

Then blue…flashes of blue, and screams like sirens… Blue flared and the wails stopped, and Freya was silent. The world was silent. Everything was still.

Freya's body jerked, once, then again…then again. Her mind did not. Her mind was free, still flying, up, up into the blue…the blue of Daddy's t-shirt, the blue that ruled the sky…

TWO
HEAVEN

There were no sudden movements, no jerk as the swing reached the top, this time Freya flew straight and free, rising all the time into the fiercest, most beautiful blue she had ever seen...

She rose and the blue became deeper, more intense, and then light diffused the colour, throwing radiance across her, warming her face and enveloping her in a feeling quite unlike anything she knew. This joy was a million times more exquisite than the heady happiness of swinging as high as she could, it didn't even match Mum's kisses or the feeling she got when Daddy wrapped his arms around her and hugged her 'til she laughed...this was something else.

Freya bathed in the light, still rising and ascending through the mirage of azure and gold. She relaxed and allowed the flow to propel her, and she somersaulted in the sky. Life surged through her veins and Freya took control. She thrust forward and upward soaring into the light.

The blend of blue and gold suffused her entire being and as she ascended the blue faded and the gold paled, until she was surrounded in pure light, white light, nothing but light. Freya felt at complete peace and threw herself on, disappearing into the brilliance, becoming part of it.

For a moment she was lost within it, where she belonged, wrapped in the most unbelievable pure peace, like being cocooned inside brand new, white cotton towels.

Then memories, memories of before, memories of life, returned and they came thick and fast, yet she comprehended every one, and as they came, her mind grew. The capacity of her awareness increased and with it all her senses sharpened. It wasn't like before…her seven-year-old mind had grown. It was like she'd been operating with an old computer, one that struggled with little virtual memory, now the cache was enormous, overflowing with information she'd always stored, but never knew how to access.

She suddenly knew the answers to a millennia of questions, mainly the "Why," and "What if," ones, questions that her parents, and philosophers, had theorised about for years! The knowledge made her grin and her little body began to shake with quiet laughter.

"I know why Daddy-long-legs exist!" She giggled. "And I know how to make rainbows!" She grinned, her eyes bright with anticipation. "I'm going to make rainbows, lots of them!"

Then clarity filled her mind, and all of a sudden reality emerged. "I'm not ready," she whispered, "I'm not ready."

Freya's eyes glazed with unshed tears and she trembled. "I think…I died…" she began, "I'm alone…" She closed her eyes, but even as she whispered she knew she wasn't alone. She could almost feel strong, yet gentle arms embracing her, comforting her, and she could almost hear a soft and melodious voice telling her to open her eyes.

She did and the glare began to fade. Salmon pink infused the light, like daybreak, and heavenly colours mingled as the brightness lessened. Pale hyacinth blue swirled within the pink, and as the dazzle disappeared her eyes immediately adjusted.

The green beneath her was the most luscious and inviting she had ever seen. The tree she now sat leaning against was shaped perfectly to offer a place to rest, and its blossom hung just low enough to enjoy its beautiful fragrance. Freya gasped, flowers nodded their heads and beautifully plumed, but tiny, birds flit to and fro, singing as if their tiny hearts depended on it.

Entranced, Freya touched the diamond-encrusted grass. Her bare toes blissfully splayed, letting blades spring through her toes and spray her feet with dew. She laughed and stood and reached up for the dripping blossom. She pulled it towards her nose and inhaled then let go, and laughed again as the bough sprang back into place.

She pirouetted, letting the white dress she was wearing whirl around her legs and then she bounded away, twirling round and round and round. When she stopped, and wasn't even dizzy, she gazed about her. She wasn't alone. She couldn't possibly be alone with all this *life* around her. Electricity charged the air and she danced towards a patch of flowers.

All the colours of the rainbow smiled up, or down, at her.

Huge yellow sunflowers, like the one she'd once planted in a paper cup at school and nurtured until it had finally bloomed in the garden, hung heavy with brown seeds as they bent their heads, and saffron-yellow petals rippled in the breeze. Love-in-the-Mist, recalled memories of scattering seeds with Mum… Freya's gaze moved over the flowers, scarlet poppies with inky black centres, her mother's favourite purply-blue roses, snow-white arum lilies, blue periwinkle interspersed with golden-orange California poppies and her favourite, bluebells, nodding their tiny flowers.

Freya's finger delicately brushed the closest lily tracing the velvety spathe, and a strange feeling stirred. She felt the flower breathe! The sensation made Freya jump. She stared at the flower and lowered her finger once more. This time she purposefully poked her finger inside the silky trumpet and didn't recoil as the flower's life force melted into her.

Freya opened her mind and allowed emotions, and simple feelings of beauty flow through her. The feelings weren't strong, or rich, just pure and simple, and Freya knew at once that all the flowers were vibrantly alive, not just with colour and scent, but with life of their own, each a simple, but divine entity.

It was then that she let the tingle of the grass beneath infuse her and she laughed again.

Her giggles filled the air and she danced away, full of life. She danced and danced, twirling this way and that, twisting beneath blossomed boughs and skipping through cherry-red poppies and bluebells. When she was done, she flopped to the ground amid the bluebells. Her hands brushed the mat of flowers and she lowered her head, staring intently at the spray of tiny bells.

They were so blue, cornflower and forget-me-not blue, bluebell blue! Their strappy leaves stood erect and strong and Freya marvelled at each intricate flower.

The detail reminded her of the High Definition adverts on television that had frustrated her dad so much. *"I haven't got an HD TV,"* he'd loudly complain, *"so how on earth am I s'posed to see the miraculous difference on the TV in the ad?"* Freya now had high definition eyes, high definition touch, high definition everything! And with that unconscious thought, came the sudden realisation, her eyesight was as clear as the proverbial bell, the scratch on her leg from the playground was gone, the tangles in her long, brown hair had vanished, she was perfect, perfect in every way.

All this was suddenly too much, Freya's fingers slipped through the flowers and her now perfect eyes lifted. She gazed about her, her mouth slightly open and a mystified expression on her face. Her brow creased and things didn't look as clear as they should.

"It's as you want it." A clear voice rang out behind her, and Freya spun round.

A small boy stood to her rear, shattering the illusion of perfection.

"A boy!" she said, barely hiding her distaste.

He grinned and nodded. "I *am* a boy." He took a step closer and Freya was up on her feet. "I'm Jake." He held out his hand.

She stayed put, her feet buried in bluebells. When she didn't respond, he continued unfazed. "It's how you like," he tried to explain, "this is your heaven. It's got your favourite things in it."

She shook her head. "So where's Purple Ted?" she asked raising her eyebrow.

"Ta da!" Jake sang, as a purple teddy bear appeared among the bluebells.

Both Freya's eyebrows rose and she crouched to reclaim her teddy from the flowerbed. She hugged him delightfully close and inhaled the bear's familiar homely smell. Unshed tears left a film across her eyes and Freya took a moment to herself. When she looked up the boy was gone.

"Where did you go?" she cried.

He stepped out of the shadows, she frowned again there were no shadows. "You wanted a moment of privacy," he told her.

She hugged Ted tight then allowed him to drop to her side in her hand. "He used to be my favourite teddy, but I'm too old for them now."

"No one's too old for teddy bears," said Jake.

She shrugged, but didn't let go of Purple Ted. "So why are you here?"

"I'm your welcoming committee, it's my turn!" He laughed and his laugh made her feel warm inside. She offered her first smile and was rewarded with a huge toothy grin. "You're my assignment!"

She bristled. "I'm no one's assignment!"

"It's okay Freya…"

"You know my name?"

"Of course!" He smiled brightly again. "I've been watching you."

"For how long?"

"Since I knew you'd be my assignment."

"I'm *not* your assignment!" she reminded him.

He flapped his arms. "I know, I know…since I knew you were *the one* then."

"And when was that?"

"When you were swinging."

"On the swing? But I wasn't dead then."

"I know! You were full of life…it's a real shame…but I was excited you were coming anyway!"

"Did you see me die?"

"Later." He waved away her question. "I'm your welcoming committee, here to help you understand heaven."

She tried a smile. "Tell me then…" She opened her arms and encompassed the meadow they stood in. "Tell me what all this is and where I am."

His smile, if it were possible, grew even brighter. "*This* is your heaven."

"You already said that."

He ignored her sarcasm. "These flowers, this garden, they're all yours."

"Mine?"

"Can't you see the flowers aren't normal? They're all flowering together even though they shouldn't be."

She hadn't noticed, but now she did. She remembered Mum's grief when the bluebells finished, but recalled how Mum always said it was sad when one season finished, but the next always brought another swathe of beauty with its own flowers. Mum loved every season, even the crunchy carpet of leaves in the autumn, and winter's snowdrops had her enthusing all over again.

Now Freya gazed across the clusters of flowers and understood, not only were the plants out of season, but each held a meaning for her.

Primroses, tiny lemon-yellow ones pushed up through the grass as she recalled how both she and her Mum preferred plants that were natural and old-fashioned. As she watched primroses surface, their tough, wrinkled leaves unfurling and thin stalks revealing buds that quickly opened, her smile deepened. She raised her hands and grinned. "Watch this!" she commanded.

She swung her hands upwards like a conductor before his orchestra and loosed her mind.

Bright orange geums burst forth, intermingled with bronze irises, more irises appeared, rising up through sword-like clumps of silver leaves, their buds unfurling to reveal huge silken flowers in an array of colours. Amongst these were black tulips, pink tulips and white tulips. Daisies the colour of butter cream, paeonies seemingly made of bowls of crinkled petals, gossamer-haired pulsatillas, pink, shaggy dianthus, the palest yellow daffodils, more roses and plum-coloured poppies.

Columbine and clematis climbed up into the trees and sweet peas twisted around trunks.

Foxgloves, verbena and sky-blue delphiniums grew tall, whilst snowdrops, cyclamen and delicate violas carpeted the woodland floor.

Jake kept his trademark grin as he sidestepped a patch of fuchsias, and avoided decapitation from a whippy willow branch, could you still get decapitated if you were already dead?

And Freya hadn't finished adding sweet-smelling philadelphus, a wine-coloured magnolia and a Christmas tree.

"Any more?" asked Jake.

She folded her arms across her chest surveying her work. "Nope, I think that's it...for now." She nodded with a broad, satisfied smile that matched Jake's and appraised her heaven. She nodded again. "It's good."

THREE
BLUEBELLS

"There's something I have to show you." Jake's face was grim, and his lack of smile alarmed Freya.

She rippled her hand through the bluebells, and closed her eyes in contemplation. When Jake didn't continue, she opened one eye and looked at him. He stared at her, unblinking, but with that same serious expression. "What?" she asked.

Jake dropped his gaze and placed a steadying hand on his knee as he moved from the grass to standing. Freya looked up at him. She didn't need to shield her eyes although the light was as bright, if not brighter, than a hot summer's day. He wore a shimmery pale blue waistcoat over a white shirt, and light brown jeans. He pushed his floppy, tawny hair away from his face and bent forward to offer his hand.

Not bothered any more about equal opportunities, she took it and stood. "So?" She met his eyes.

He gave a deep sigh and shook his head. "This is the bit I wasn't really looking forward to, but no one can get away from it."

"What does?"

"We need to go and see something."

"Where?"

"Okay, we don't need to *go* anywhere, it's a figure of speech. But let's move somewhere quiet." He gently tugged her hand.

"This isn't quiet enough?" she asked with a small grin. All she could hear was the hum of bees and the birds' soft twitter.

"Humour me. Let's just move away a bit." Jake led her out of the woodland and across the green sward to a huge weeping willow.

As they sat beneath its quivering boughs, Freya giggled. "A weeping willow and no water, I'll have to do something about that…"

Jake put his hand over hers as she began to move her hands in a fluid movement. "The water will have to wait."

"Okay, so what now, what's so important?"

"This is." Jake closed his eyes.

"Do I close my eyes too?"

"Just for a moment," he instructed in no more than a whisper. "Freya, think of your family…"

"My family?"

"Just think of them then open your eyes."

Freya closed her eyes. At first she could think of nothing but the garden surrounding her, the glory of pulling flowers out of nowhere… then nothing, her mind went blank and try as she might she could not see her family. "I can't…" she said peeping at the boy beside her.

"Just relax…" whispered Jake.

She squeezed her eyes shut and thought hard, still nothing… then the barrier dropped, like sluice gates, slowly but surely, and there they were, her family.

They sat in a chapel, with a small white casket before them. The casket was covered in blue. Masses of bluebells were strewn across it, and Mum still clutched a limp bunch in her white hands.

Bluebells and tears. Freya stared in silence. Bluebells and tears were all she could see.

The cream-coloured chapel walls encompassed a congregation full of grief. The teal-green carpet enhanced the white coffin, and the walnut pulpit was decorated with sprays of spring flowers. Someone had spent time and effort filling baskets with primroses, gypsophelia, more bluebells and tiny creamy-yellow roses. Freya stared, and the first thought that came to her was that the roses were out of season. This confused her for a moment, was this still heaven?

Then her glance moved back to her family and her little heart broke.

Her parents sat together, both in black, Dad in his Sunday suit and Mum in a familiar black skirt, but a new black top, something Freya did not recognise. The new wrap top suited her mother, whereas the tears that streamed down her face did not.

Jasmine wriggled in Granddad's arms, struggling to reach her father sitting so close, yet so far. Grandma was out in the foyer trying to arrange a small group of children, trying to keep her own sorrow in check whilst she supported her daughter. Freya's other Grandparents sat behind their son, her Grandfather's hand resting on her father's shoulder, wishing he could help when he couldn't.

Grandma herded in the children, the organ struck up and they sang, and Freya sang along.

"They're singing for me," she whispered, "for me."

When they sat down the Minister stood at the pulpit, even his eyes were red-rimmed, but he spoke with a solid voice, one that did not crack like her primary teacher's did.

Her schoolteacher spoke of Freya's joy for life, her intelligence, her fun-loving mind, and her friends.

Her friends sat by their parents, not all had come, some parents thought services like this were too much for ones so young to bear, but Freya smiled at those who had come. Her friends sat there, stiff and quiet, in awe of the occasion. One or two of the boys had let their minds wander and one was studying a spider crawling up the side of the pulpit.

Her best friend, Meg, stared at the coffin, and swung her legs to and fro. Meg liked the flowers and nodded to herself in approval at the bluebells. She leaned close to her mother and whispered. "Is she in there?"

Meg's mother glanced down mortified at her daughter's question, but relieved that it had been whispered, a child not so well brought up might have said it out loud…that was too much to consider. Her mother nodded twice, and put her finger to her lips. It didn't prevent Meg's second murmured query. "Is she coming back?" This time Meg's mother turned to look at her daughter. She saw the wide brown eyes stare back at her and she struggled to maintain her composure. She glanced at the casket and then back to her own daughter. As she shook her head in answer, she bit her lip, some things were just too awful to consider, and her heart, among many others in the congregation, broke for Freya's parents.

Freya couldn't look at her parents, she couldn't hold the emotions that threatened to overwhelm her, so she searched the chapel again, who had come to see her go?

Her neighbours, Donald and Daisy, how she had laughed when they'd told her their names. "Like the ducks?" she'd howled. "Yes, like the ducks!" They'd grinned. They sat quietly, holding hands, Daisy clasping a fresh white handkerchief.

Several teenagers sat together, one of them, holding a single white rose, twirling it back and forth in her fingers. Her two girl friends sniffed together, trying to hold back their tears. The boys looked uncomfortable, but smart in their crisp, freshly laundered white shirts.

Her Headmaster sat beside two of her teachers, and was surrounded by school friends and their families.

Mrs French, the widowed postmistress mopped her eyes, and shared a whispered word with Jen, her daughter who sat at the till.

The postman was there, so was the nurse that lived across the road, the neighbours from two doors up, and three doors up, and four, next door the other-side…neighbours she'd never even seen before were there.

Several parents occupied the small chapel nursery, and listened amid their toddlers chatter to the service on the radio feed to the room.

One or two babies slept in their pushchairs with their mothers at the back of the chapel.

The Hillmans sat up near the front, listening quietly. Thomas Hillman refused to release his wife's hand throughout; he knew how frail mortality was.

Singing erupted again, joyous music rising up through the rafters, ascending to Freya herself…

Freya watched the chorister, a young girl who thought herself far too young and inexperienced to be conducting the hymns for this most beautiful of services. Her hands trembled but Freya smiled.

Bishop Williams rose again and shared his own thoughts on Freya, including the funny story of when she'd hidden after church and was only discovered, her little face covered with panic-stricken tears pressed against the foyer door, after the chapel's alarm had been set! Some people laughed as they remembered her, many allowed tears to roll down their faces. Freya chuckled.

Freya blinked and caught Jake's face beside her. "Is this normal?" she asked, "Can I laugh at my own funeral?"

"You can do whatever you want," he replied, "I've seen people laugh, cry, have hysterics…and I've seen people who have no reaction at all."

"Did you see your own?"

He nodded then held up his hand to stop her next question. "Wait…watch this bit." He looked down intently. "I'm not being horrible here, but we have bets about this bit…"

"What bit?" Freya asked, intrigued.

She stared down and watched the organist fiddle with a CD player.

"The song…" Jake paused. The chords to a familiar song began and Jake grinned and slapped his knee quietly. "'Angels'…" He smiled at Freya. "It's the one we all know by heart!"

"So do I, it's one of my favourites," replied Freya remembering long car trips. "We always sing it loud, me, Mum and Dad, even Jasmine tries to join in!"

"Then sing…" said Jake.

Freya did. Below her parents gripped hands, and her mother's tears watered the bluebells in her lap. The congregation in church listened as the words and music filled the chapel…and Freya sang.

And as Freya sang, and her father mouthed the words, Jake began to sing, and accompanying Jake rose a heavenly choir. Freya turned, still singing, and watched as her meadow filled with children, children her age and younger, children dressed in rainbow colours and white. They sang and even Robbie Williams struggled to be heard.

Down below the children in church looked up, Jasmine stopped grizzling, and Freya's parents glanced at each other, stirred by the music. For years after, the congregation would swear blind that they had heard angels, real ones, just for a split second during that song.

FOUR
WHITE ROSES

The graveside was a more sombre affair; even Freya didn't feel like singing. Most of the congregation had cried their tears and said their goodbyes at the chapel. The cemetery was a family gathering. Uncle Pete had turned up late, but that had been expected, he wasn't much of a churchgoer. He'd left his bike down by the Chapel of Rest and walked the length of the cemetery with his helmet tucked under his arm. His leathers creaked as he joined the silent group, but his sister reached out and touched his gloved hand in gratitude.

Freya yearned to leap into his arms, she closed her eyes and remembered how Uncle Pete would catch her, hug her then spin her round and round…

Uncle Pete placed his motorcycle helmet on the ground, peeled off his gloves and moved beside his parents. He nodded and the Minister opened his scriptures.

Freya watched as her closest family stood around her grave. She saw Jasmine whimper in Gran's arms and reach again for her father, but Gran clucked softly to soothe her. Grandpa stroked Jasmine's curly hair, but kept a stiff expression on his face. Beside them stood her parents, side-by-side, hands gripped in grief. Then stood Grandma and Granddad, and behind them was the shadowy bulk of Uncle Pete.

Freya didn't listen to the words that flew around her grave; she turned her attention to her parents instead.

They both stared down into the grave, at the white box covered with bluebells. Tears no longer fell from her mother's eyes, but grey streaks stained her cheeks. Her husband gripped her hand so hard her fingers were white, but she did not notice, or maybe the pain was comforting in some strange way. She still held the bluebells in her other hand but the stems were squashed and the flowers were stressed.

Freya's father stood firm, his feet planted in the grass, his lower lip quivering, but his eyes never left the coffin in the ground.

Grandma held a sheaf of nine roses, pure white rosebuds, in the crook of her arm, and as silence fell she gently released the lilac ribbon tied loosely around the stems, and handed one to each of the relatives. She was left with two. "For Anna, who couldn't be here today," she said, speaking of her absent daughter, as she dropped the rose into the grave.

Up above, Freya left the graveside and spied across the ocean. Aunty Anna was quiet. It was dawn in the part of Canada where she lived, and she sat on a wooden bench in her garden, hugged in a fleece to keep out the snowy chill. She held a single white rose in her hand and thought of her three children asleep in bed only moments away from her.

Grandma then released her own rose and moved to allow her husband to do the same. Uncle Pete shook his head and a tear slipped down into the hole with his flower.

"And me!" came a plea from Jasmine, "And mine fower!" she cried.

Gran stepped forward and Jasmine threw her rose with gusto. Gran's dropped beside it, as did Grandpa's.

Freya's Mum glanced up at her husband. He nodded then dropped to his knees, a choked sob left his throat and his daughter's name with it. "Freya…" he croaked, "Oh Freya…" His wife bent and touched his shoulder, but that only made his pain worse. His sobs echoed across the tombstones and Freya watched as her mother took him in her arms. They knelt together, his tears spilling onto the grass, until he wiped them away and his wife softly spoke his name. "Joe…say goodbye…"

He sniffed and cleared his throat, a thunderous noise in the solitude and silence of the cemetery, and got back up onto his feet. "Freya," he whispered, "goodbye, I love you." And he cast his white rose into the grave. "Rachel?" he said and his wife took his hand as he helped her stand.

"I know," she said, "but I don't know if I can…"

He kissed her wet cheek. "It's not forever," he whispered.

Rachel stared first up into the sky, and Freya gazed down at her intense stare and wondered, for a moment, if her mother could see right into heaven, then she looked down and tried to focus on the casket in the earth. She bit her lip and gripped the rose so tight that a stray thorn, that hadn't been removed in the florist's careful check, pierced her finger. She began to shiver, as if an icy wind had chilled her, and her teeth chattered. It suddenly all began to feel surreal and Rachel wondered for a moment why she was even there. Surely seven-year-old daughters don't die? She'd go home to find her playing, riding up and down the road on her purple bicycle…then she remembered and her tears began again.

"My little Freya…" she wept, "goodbye my little baby." She let the rose slip through her fingers and turned away. As the rosebud's soft thud echoed on the casket Freya's family walked away across the emerald grass.

"I need white roses." Freya jumped to her feet.

Jake leaped up too and grabbed hold of her. "Wait," he said, as she struggled against his grip. "Just wait."

"I need roses, white ones!" she cried, and as she did brambles appeared pushing through the grass, no, not brambles, but rose bushes. Thorn-less rose stems erupted, thickening into bushes, and as they grew buds appeared and the swollen buds burst open into luscious white flowers.

Jake released his hold and let Freya drop to the floor, just as her father had. "White roses…white roses…" she sobbed.

Soon the roses were everywhere, spreading across the meadow and Freya's sobs turned into quiet moans. "They gave me white roses."

Jake crouched beside her and put his arms around her shoulders, and there they sat until Freya had run out of tears.

As Freya recovered she lifted her tear-streaked face to Jake. "Is it always that hard?"

He let out a little laugh and ignored her injured expression. "At least you only ever have to go through it once!"

She managed a small smile. "So that was my funeral."

He nodded.

"So, I'm well and truly dead then?"

He nodded again.

"Well, I'd better get used to it then." She slowly stood gazing about her. "Did I really make *all* these roses?"

He nodded.

She allowed herself a little laugh. "I don't think I need that many!"

As she whispered the bushes began to shrivel and disappear, and soon only a small bed remained surrounding the willow.

She cupped a single rose in her hand and studied the dewdrop confined in the centre, like a stolen tear. "I'll never forget…white roses."

FIVE
ANGELS

When Freya met the other children, the ones who had out sung Robbie at her funeral, she was a little upset to discover none were flitting around heaven using traditional, bulky, but beautifully feathered, angel wings. In fact she was more than a little peeved when no one explained how she could acquire such wings at all!

Jake laughed, and not only laughed but actually collapsed holding his sides with laughter, when she requested wings.

"Wings!" He wiped his eyes. "What d'you want wings for?"

"To fly," she said indignantly.

"Tell me..." he began, "what do they teach you down there?"

"That there are *angels* in heaven and they *have* wings!"

When Jake guffawed again Freya spun on her heels, crossed her arms over her chest and flounced away.

"Sorry...Freya," Jake chuckled, "I'm sorry..."

"Hmmph." Freya continued walking.

"I am sorry, really," Jake's voice softened, "I s'pose it's an easy mistake!"

"*Mis-take?*" Freya turned back to him. "Angels on earth have wings. They do in pictures, and on Christmas trees..."

"And in Michelangelo's paintings…all chubby cherubs, curly hair and cute feathers," finished Jake. "Like I said, easy mistake."

"So I won't get wings?" Freya still looked annoyed. "Or a halo?"

"Why would you need wings?"

"To fly." Freya had always fancied flying hence her enjoyment of swinging so much.

Jake shook his head with a wry smile. "Right, it's time for a few more revelations then," he told her. "The children you've met, the other children here…where do you think they come from? And do they look like chubby cherubs?"

A small frown crossed Freya's face as she considered. She shook her head. "I don't know." She gazed across the meadow as far as she could see. "Where did they come from, and more to the point where are they now?"

"One at a time," said Jake. "Okay, let's start at the beginning…" He took a deep breath. "When you first arrive everything is new, and you get a guide…moi," He twirled his finger and pointed at himself with a flourish. "We help you settle, make sure you know what's happened and stay with you while you learn where you are."

Freya nodded.

"At first, while you get used to the idea of…"

"Death." Freya finished for him.

"Death…" Jake continued, "You're in a place that *you* make. You made a garden." Again Jake swept out his arms indicating the mass of flowers illustrating his words. "One little boy recreated his bedroom, another lived in his dog's kennel for ages…one girl even made a theme park! You made a garden…but although your garden will always be here, you will move on."

"Where to?"

Jake smiled. "I don't know, *I'm* not ready yet."

"When will you be ready?" asked Freya.

Jake shrugged.

"When will I be ready?" she asked.

He shrugged again. "We're all told we'll know when we're ready."

Neither spoke for a few moments then Jake took Freya's arm. "Look." He pointed into the woods. Behind a tree, badly hidden, was a child; badly hidden, because a sparkly skirt flared out either side of the thin tree. Freya laughed, and her laughter made the girl tilt her head. She caught Freya's glance and smiled back, she smoothed down her skirt and edged away from the tree. As she did several others revealed themselves and soon a whole troupe of children emerged from the woods.

Freya was delighted, and her delight grew as they wandered through her garden complimenting the planting!

Very soon she tugged at Jake's sleeve. "Okay, so why am I the only one wearing a plain white dress?"

At first Freya had loved her simple, floaty dress, it fit so well, there were no annoying, itchy labels, no zips or buttons, no too-tight or too-loose elastic, nothing but a perfect fit. But now she noticed that the other girls' dresses were either shimmery, or lacy, or longer, and they were all coloured. There were no bright, bold colours, nothing like the flowers she'd produced, but rainbows had splashed all the dresses nonetheless.

"Why is mine plain white?" she repeated.

"You can choose…you just haven't done it yet," Jake told her.

"Where do I choose, where are they kept?"

"You're wearing it, look." A little girl a year or two younger than Freya lightly touched her arm.

Freya glanced down and sucked in her breath. She'd been admiring the bodice of another girl, the colour of moonlight and covered in tiny silver stars. Now as she stared down at her chest she was wearing the same top. "I can change it? Wow! Just like this!" She turned it from silvery-lemon to pink. "Wow!"

Suddenly all the girls were altering their dresses! Skirts were flickering from pale-blue to pastel-pink, to soft gold and mint, and back again. Sleeves were floaty and short, then long and slender, and all the girls gathered in a huddle.

One or two boys changed the colour of their waistcoat, but generally the boys had no interest in the fashion-show frenzy.

Freya finally settled on a hint of lilac, the bodice developed hooks and eyes and a silver ribbon, and the skirt, long and flared, reached her calves. Freya twirled and twirled and relished the admiration of the girls. Finally she flopped to the floor beside Jake.

"Are you finished?" he asked with a grin.

She nodded, totally oblivious of his boredom. "So, still no wings?" She looked hopeful. "I can't just magic them up myself, can I?"

He shook his head. "That brings me back to my original point…you don't need them." He ignored her frustrated sigh. "You really don't. Everyone here just chose to be here, to come and see you, no one had to fly, they just decided."

"They just decided to be here and…"

"And they were." Jake nodded.

Freya thought for a moment then knowledge flashed through her mind and a big smile spread across her face. "I can just think things and they'll happen?"

Jake nodded again.

Freya was back up on her feet in a second. She stood on tiptoes again and pirouetted then flopped back down. "But I still can't have wings?"

This time Jake shook his head.

Up again and Freya's smile contained a hint of mischief. "Anywhere?" she asked and was gone. Jake's head whipped round and he spied her at the rear of the pack of girls. Then she was gone again. It took a moment before he spotted her peering out from behind a particularly large Hebe. He got to his feet and was beside her in flash. "See, I can do it too." He grinned.

She disappeared again, but he was with her, and she led him a merry dance across her meadow, finishing at the weeping willow. She dropped to the ground again her eyes twinkling. "This is amazing!" She sucked in a big breath, and blew up her cheeks and exhaled. "Wow!" she said, "I'm dead...I think I'm an angel, but without wings...I can make flowers and trees...and change my clothes without undressing! I can get anywhere I want by just thinking about it..." She tapped her skull. "*And* there is so much more in *there* than there ever was before!"

She got to her feet again and wandered towards the willow trunk. The tree towered over her, the trunk bending beneath the weight of its boughs. Feathery leaves fluttered and Freya ran her fingers through the fronds. She sighed again. "This is amazing."

Her gaze travelled and took her to her roses. Then she was beside them, bending her neck to plunge her nose into satiny petals. She inhaled deeply, letting the sweet fragrance intoxicate her. She closed her eyes and let memories wash over her.

She remembered her mother's purple roses. 'Rhapsody in Blue...could there ever be a better name for a rose?' Her mother had said as they'd admired the colour. 'And they smell good!' Freya had laughed. That day Freya had pulled a petal from the rose and sat on the grass rubbing it between her thumb and forefinger. It felt soft, velvety, and safe. Safe was a strange emotion to be contained within a rose, but it was actually the garden that made Freya feel safe. Her mother's domain, her mother's favourite place and that made it equally Freya's favourite place.

While her mother dug, weeded, planted, watered and watched her plants grow, Freya watched her mother. The flowers became her companions, the snails, and ladybirds and butterflies her playmates, and the garden her kingdom.

Now Freya touched the pale rose in her hand and stroked a petal, allowing the sentiment to take her back to earth, back to her garden, back to her mother... Overwhelmed, Freya opened her eyes and her smile vanished.

Jake placed his hand on her shoulder and patted it lightly.

"Anywhere?" she murmured, "I can go anywhere?"

"Anywhere," he whispered, "but not there."

SIX
PURPLE TED

The garden was just as she'd left it. Her bike resting against the shed, the front wheel turned in, and the white wicker basket still holding the plastic cups and saucers Freya had been playing with. The only thing missing was Purple Ted, he no longer sat in the basket, he now sat indoors, upstairs, on Mum's pillow.

The weeks had overtaken her parents and no one had thought to put her bike away. It remained outside getting wetter with every rainy day.

"It'll rust," thought Freya pragmatically as she stared down at it.

Freya was on her own, drawn to her special place below, but unable to reach it.

Beneath her, at home, the bluebells were finishing, their strappy leaves faded and yellow, beside them lily-of-the-valley tried its best to last a few more days.

Taking over were the spiky blue clumps of dianthus, already in flower and intoxicating anyone who bent close with their delicious, heavy fragrance. The newer, smaller clumps were Freya's. She'd spent months last summer watching several little pots of cuttings, getting excited every time a new, green pair of spiky leaves emerged from the centre of the sprig. The shoots thrived and in the autumn, when they were strong and bushy, Freya had planted them. Now their silver-blue foliage was the perfect foil to the dainty, pink flowers, every petal cut by fairies' pinking shears…

"Fairies!" Freya chuckled. "They exist no more than chubby, renaissance angels!"

She could see each flower as if she were knelt beside it, and the scent rose, spiralling a million miles, or so, until she could smell it too. Her lip curled into a wry smile. "Memory…" her mind affirmed, "I can see it, but the smell is from memory."

The back door suddenly swung open and Freya's mum stepped outside. She stood for a moment then the small girl clambering down the step behind her grabbed her attention. "Careful…" She spoke softly and held out her hand to steady the toddler.

"Jasmine," Freya breathed.

The little girl clutched a pale-blue teddy in her fist and dropped it as she stood outside beside her mother. "Ooops Ted," she said in a singsong voice and bent to pick him up. "Dere, dere." She patted him soothingly.

Freya's mum didn't move, but watched wistfully as her youngest daughter trotted across the yard. Jasmine, oblivious to the two sets of eyes on her, reached the glittery-violet bicycle. The handlebars shone in the sun and Jasmine swung her teddy bear by her side. She stood for a moment staring at the bike. Rachel, her mother, opened her mouth but didn't speak. Jasmine nodded to herself and lifted up her teddy; she kissed him and plonked him unceremoniously into the plastic basket.

Rachel lifted her hand, and grief filled her eyes, but again she did not speak. She let her hand drop to her side and sank down onto the back door step. Jasmine waddled away from the bike and back towards Mum. She beamed at Mum and then pushed past behind her, disappearing back into the house.

Teddy peered over the edge of the bicycle basket, a permanent smile sewed in place, and ignored the tears that streamed down Rachel's face.

Freya's mother didn't get further than the back door that day.

An hour later it began to rain and Rachel disappeared back into the house. Then Jasmine climbed back down the step and toddled to the bike. "Ted wet," she said and reached up to yank him back into her arms. "Dere, dere," she sang, and carried him tenderly indoors.

Freya's gaze broke through the brick walls, and through the interior partitions, and she watched her sister as she scrambled up onto her parents' bed. Jasmine cuddled into her mother and cradled her teddy bear as her mother cradled Purple Ted, both bears wet with rain and tears.

SEVEN
THERE

"I wanted to touch her…" Freya sat, despondent, beneath the willow.

Jake wore a concerned expression. "I know, but you can't."

"I don't see why not, I only want to…be there."

"But you can't."

"I know, you've already told me." Freya frowned. A light mist had descended in her heaven, which matched her mood. "But I still don't see why not. It would help."

"Who would it help, you or your Mum?"

"Both."

"D'you think?"

She nodded. "I just want to hug her, to be with her. I want to go home." Freya's shoulders slumped. "I want to go home, Jake, I want to go home now." Her eyes teared up as she looked at him.

"But you only just got here…"

She shrugged. "It's nice and all, but I want to go now, I want to go home."

Jake stared wordlessly at her, unsure how to react. "But there's so much more to see…" he started lamely.

"I don't want to see any more."

"Of course you do!" He fixed a smile on his face and jumped to his feet. "C'mon..." He held out his hand.

Freya crossed her arms and her frown grew deeper still.

"C'mon..." he pleaded.

"I don't want to go, I want to go home! I want my Mum." She closed her eyes and refused to look at him.

Jake hopped from one foot to the other, his head spinning, *his first assignment and he was going to blow it!* "Please Freya... come with me."

Hot tears overflowed and with them Freya released little choked sobs. Jake's eyes opened wide with panic, and he dropped to his knees. "C'mon Freya, don't cry."

Her eyes flew open and she looked up at him beseechingly. "Then tell me how to get home!"

His voice was barely more than a whisper. "You *are* home."

"I'm not, *look*!"

Freya fell forward onto all fours and before them heaven slipped away. She gazed down at the scene that opened. It was nothing special, just a mother and a father watching television, sitting side-by-side on a sofa with a toddler playing at their feet.

The soap on screen failed to hold their attention, and gossip filled the room, but nobody heard it.

Freya's father tightened his lips as his wife leaned into his shoulder. She snuggled close, her hair slipping across her face. She absently flicked it back and watched Jasmine on the floor. Jasmine chattered, as only toddlers do, and then climbed up onto her father's lap. He hooked his arm around his small daughter and held her close. Jasmine wriggled free and sat upright. She squirmed as he grabbed her and tickled her. Her laughter filled the room and her parents' hearts burned with love.

Rachel remained tucked into her husband's side while Jasmine struggled to contain her giggles. Suddenly Joe stopped tickling her and pulled her to him close, Jasmine did not resist. With difficulty he kept his composure, whilst he clasped his daughter and held his wife.

All eyes focused on the television, though the screen was nothing but a blur.

"I want to be there," Freya whispered.

Jake shrugged cheerlessly, while Freya's heart sprouted wings of its own and left.

Freya followed her heart.

In a whoosh of cold air she was there.

She stood in the same room as her family. Nothing had changed, Jasmine still sat enveloped in her father's arms, her mother was motionless, her hand resting on Joe's arm as he held her, and her father still stared blankly at the television screen.

Freya didn't move she held her position so still a statue would have been envious. Nothing happened.

The television continued to blare, soap actresses still shouted at each other, theme music boomed into the quiet room and Freya could contain herself no longer.

"I'm here!" she cried and her voice caught with emotion. "I'm here."

The bulb above her flickered, as did the television, and the stereo clock began to blink.

"I'm here!" she shouted and clasped her hands to her chest.

Nobody moved, nobody shivered, or flinched or even started.

"I'm here…" Freya's voice disappeared as she sank to her knees. "Flicker, lights please…" she begged. "Do it again and show them I'm here."

Her family remained fused together on the sofa, oblivious of anything but each other.

Freya stayed on her knees and watched them. Her mother closed her eyes, and her father pursed his lips even tighter. He stared straight at Freya, with a gaze so intent, she could do nothing but return it. His stare was empty of sight, his eyes glazed with unshed tears, and Freya desperately wanted to know what he was feeling. There was no way to penetrate his mind, no way to see what he was seeing behind the blindness. His fingers gripped Jasmine's arm leaving little indents from each finger. The tips of his fingers got whiter until suddenly Jasmine cried out and shook his hand away.

"I'm sorry!" Joe snapped back into reality and immediately rubbed his daughter's arm, apologising readily until she smiled and hugged him back.

The moment was broken.

Rachel swung her feet up onto the sofa and leaned away from Joe, slumping into the cushion and slipping her toes beneath Joe's thigh. Jasmine grinned at her father then slipped off his lap back down to her toys at his feet.

Joe sighed and glanced at his wife. "Bedtime then?"

She nodded and began to stretch.

"No, let me do it." Joe put his hand on her leg to stay her. "C'mon Jazzy, let's go, kiss your Mum."

Jasmine leapt into her mother's arms and planted a big kiss on her cheek, then an even bigger one on her lips. Mum laughed and wrapped her arms around her little girl. Both were lost in the hug until Dad spoke again. "C'mon Jaz."

Jasmine slipped off mum and grabbed Teddy from the floor. She took her father's hand and allowed him to lead her from the room, giving a huge yawn as she disappeared through the door. "Bye, bye, Mummy."

"Bye, bye Jasmine," replied Mum.

Joe closed the door behind him and Freya was alone in the room with her Mum.

Rachel reached for the remote control and switched off the television. The silence was consuming. Freya relaxed into a lotus position on the floor and watched her mother. Rachel stared at her fingers for a long time, tugging at the quick on her forefinger, before eventually biting off the offending scrap of skin. She ran her fingers over her cheek, and across her lips, as if trying to retrace the kisses left there by Jasmine. Then she began to chew a fingernail and her eyes travelled across the room.

They didn't settle on Freya sat in front of her, but on Freya's image opposite on the mantel.

It was her favourite photograph of her daughter. One she'd taken in the woods behind the house. Freya was wearing fairy wings; you couldn't really see them, because her face filled the frame, but they were there, gauzy and lilac behind her dark hair. She'd been dancing through the trees, singing and chattering, and Rachel had followed with the camera poised for what seemed like ages…then Freya turned and in that split second Rachel caught her, froze the moment of magic forever.

Freya's upturned nose was creased as her mouth formed a huge, open smile and her green, pixie eyes twinkled as the sun sparkled. Both innocence and mischief were captured on the little girl's face, melded together, and Rachel loved the picture.

Joe had suggested it was the photo they should give to the police, the one that got shown on the news and the one that depicted Freya forever in the papers, but Rachel refused. She didn't want that picture tainted, didn't want it connected in any way with her death, so the traditional school photo had been the one that found its way on to the television and newspapers. It wasn't even this photograph that appeared in the chapel at the funeral, this one was special; this one belonged to Freya and Rachel, Joe and Jasmine.

She stared at the image and smiled. Then she let the silent tears loose and allowed them to slip down her cheeks unchecked.

Freya watched.

When Joe came back in, he glanced at his wife and carefully shut the door. He gently sat down and took her in his arms.

"It was the photo…" she began.

"I know, I know…"

He held her as she wept, and his tears mingled with hers.

Freya breathed slowly and quietly, until it occurred to her that she wasn't breathing at all. Her body was still doing what she expected, although it no longer needed to. It was a strange sensation to not breathe, but as natural as breathing itself. Instead she listened to her parents' ragged breaths until they had both cried themselves out.

The room was silent except for the odd sigh and sniff, and her parents relaxed their hold on each other. Joe pulled himself up in his chair and held out his arm, as before, so Rachel could lean close and he could wrap it around her shoulder. They settled and Rachel closed her eyes.

Freya's soul, she now knew it wasn't her heart anymore, yearned to reach them. She, very slowly, got to her feet and stood before them. "I'm here…" she whispered once more then she carefully, almost reverently, climbed up onto her father's lap.

She traced her mother's cheek with her finger and placed a tiny kiss on her father's. Then she closed her eyes and curled her ghostly form between them.

She was there.

EIGHT
SLIP

When her parents went to bed, Freya did not follow them. She, instead, drifted home. *Home...* she was torn, how would she ever define 'home' again?

"What did you expect?" asked Jake softly, almost bitterly. "I told you you couldn't go back."

"I know." Her voice was barely above a whisper. "I just...I just wanted to go back, to be in their arms... I made the lights flicker!"

"No you didn't. It was an advert break, the programme finished, your flickering light was only a power surge..."

Freya's face dropped, and Jake put his arm round her shoulder. "Did it help?"

"No, yes...I don't know."

They sat quietly among the willow fronds and it seemed like an age before Freya spoke again. "Yes, it helped, I was with them. I was there."

"Will you do it again?"

"Probably."

Silence.

"Do you ever go back?" she asked Jake.

After another long pause Jake replied. "Not now."

"Did you?"

"Of course I did, maybe that's why I didn't want you to go."

"Why?" Freya turned toward him.

"I didn't want you to feel like I did." He dipped his head to hide his expression.

Freya considered his reply for a moment then asked. "How did you die?"

"Drowned,"

"Where?"

"In our pool."

"In your *pool*, what *swimming* pool?" She raised her eyebrows.

"Yes."

"Oh, I thought you meant in a pond or something, your swimming pool? Were you rich?"

He shrugged.

Freya continued. "Did you go back after? Did you see your parents?"

He nodded.

"And?"

"And what?" He turned back to her with a strangled voice. "*And* what?"

She watched him pensively. "You said you didn't want me to feel like you did."

"I don't."

"So what happened?" she asked softly.

"When I died, I slipped, hit my head and knew nothing about it."

"An accident too," she said, "just like me."

"No!" The violence in his voice made her jump. "Not like yours." His face darkened. "Nothing like yours. I watched you run out in front of that car…there wasn't anything you or anyone else could do about it. Yours was an accident."

"Did someone push you?"

"No, nothing like that."

"Then it was an accident."

"But I wasn't meant to be there," his voice wavered. "Mum wasn't well, I should've been indoors. I ignored her, wanted to play in the pool..."

"And you slipped."

"Yes, I slipped, but that wasn't the end of it."

Freya met his eyes. "Go on."

"I drowned, I don't remember how, not even now." He brushed his fringe from his eyes and paused. "You know you asked if we were rich?" She nodded. "Well we were. We were rich in all the things that didn't matter. After I'd gone, Dad tried to help Mum cope. He did everything he could, bought her everything, but he couldn't buy her out of this one. A year to the day I drowned, she followed me into the water."

Freya drew in her breath.

"She never got out again."

"Is she here?" Freya was wide-eyed.

"No."

"Where then?"

"She's still there."

"Where?"

"By the pool, she's dead and she sits by the pool, trapped by it. Dad remarried. It's funny really, he and his new wife still live there, *with her!*"

"Why is she still down there?"

He shrugged. "I did go back once, when she was alive, but her guilt was too painful. *She* felt guilty, so guilty, and I did too and it tore me up, broke my heart." Jake shook his head. "So I didn't go back again, not even after she died. I watched all the time, I watched Dad at her funeral and the months after, I had to. I couldn't *do* anything, but if anything happened to him as well, it was bad enough I was the reason she died, but for him too..."

Jake paused. "She didn't go back until after the funeral, so like you, she probably wanted to see him again, only she never left. She's still there."

"How old were you when you died?" asked Freya.

"Same as you, seven."

"Was that long ago?"

"She's been there for about five years."

"That long!" Freya was surprised. "You still look seven, the same as me, but you should be a teenager by now!"

"I'll stay seven until I'm ready." He didn't look at her.

"Jake, that's too long not to be *ready*," she began and reached towards him. She gently touched his chin and brought him round to face her. "Jake, surely you should be ready by now?"

"Probably."

"How long do we stay here?"

"Like I said, until we're ready." He stared into her eyes. "Some are ready right away, especially the babies. For some it only takes a short while, and for others it takes longer. You probably won't be here long," he added.

"You should go back and see her," said Freya.

"I can't."

"You should."

Jake rocked onto his knees and stood up. "I can't." He shook his head and walked away. Freya made a move to stand but he was gone and she was left alone staring into her bluebell wood.

There was somewhere she needed to be.

NINE
RIPPLES

One thought was all it needed.

One thought and there she was standing on the edge of an oval swimming pool. Freya looked around her and smiled to herself. He'd been wrong, there was no one here. Then Freya looked again, and on the far side of the pool was a woman, she sat with her feet in the water, kicking lazily, but no splash accompanied her kicks. The water was still across the whole pool, as still as it was beneath her feet.

Jake's Mum, Jake's ghost of a mother, sat peering into the water, her arms stretched by her sides and her hands flat on the tiled poolside. She wore a simple white dress, not unlike the one Freya had worn, only it was more elegant. With her head bent and wavy fair hair framing her face, she looked like a woman with no care in the world.

No care, that was, until she raised her face to the sun. Freya whistled between her teeth. Haunted wasn't even the right word to describe the pain etched into her young and beautiful features.

Freya raised a hesitant hand, but knew that the woman would never respond. Instead she wandered slowly around the pool until she reached Jake's mother. She stood beside the woman and crouched, then sat on the edge with her.

Freya dipped her feet into the pool too, and allowed herself a smile. She couldn't feel the water, but again memories made up for the lack of a sense of touch. Her feet kicked the water and she could feel water splashing up her legs as she closed her eyes. When she opened them again she half expected the woman to have disappeared, but she hadn't. She still sat, sunlight glinting in her glossy hair, staring into the pool.

"Jake…" the woman murmured, "My Jake…"

Freya tilted her head. She didn't need to shield her eyes from the glare of the sun, as her eyes no longer had need for such sensitivities. "He's not here," she said.

"Jake…" his mother repeated.

This woman did not exist, Freya could not imagine where she really was, but she was not in her world, neither was she among the living. Freya moved her hand to cover the pale hand on the poolside, but there was nothing there. Jake's mother faded and was gone.

The only ripple was not of water but her words as they faded with her. "Jake…my Jake…"

TEN
RAINBOWS

Freya wandered through her bluebells searching for Jake. She discovered him sitting hunched beneath her willow. Melancholy hung in a veil of mist as she approached. She waved it away and tugged Jake's arm. He offered a watery smile, but couldn't hide the delight in his eyes when she grinned back. He held out his hand and Freya pulled him to his feet, dragging him out from under the long, green fronds.

"So when can I make a rainbow?" She needed to draw him out of his depression and that's what rainbows were for.

"Anytime you like," he replied.

Freya swung her arms over her head and drew a rainbow in the sky.

"It's as easy as that...*up here*," he told her.

Freya smiled at her rainbow, it was just the right shape, a perfect arc, and the colours were, well, perfect. Its scarlet outer bow was just the right pillar-box red and the orange was joyful as was its sunshine-yellow. Green the colour of grass, then the blue, like Daddy's t-shirt, gave way to dark indigo and it all faded into the most beautiful violet to finish.

She glanced over at Jake. "What d'you mean 'easy, up here'?"

"Just that, it's easy up here, but not so easy down there."

"Huh, I make perfect rainbows, look!"

"Yes, *up here*."

Freya continued to glare at him with her arms folded tight across her chest.

"Up here, you don't need anything, down there you need the right conditions," he began to explain.

"What d'you mean?"

"It needs to be rainy and sunny."

"So, I just choose the right day then."

Jake shrugged. "I s'pose."

But the right day did not appear.

For a while Freya gave up on rainbows, they appeared in the sky regularly, but none of them belonged to her.

Her attempt at a birthday rainbow for her mother was almost non-existent, because the sun shone with such intensity that all she produced was a pale arc in a vapoury sky that amounted to nothing.

The science of rainbows left her somewhat defeated, she knew she had to influence the light and she knew she contained enough inherent celestial light to create a small rainbow, but it was the rain that had her beaten. It had to be in the right place and she had to use the existing sunlight to enhance her own fragile light. Dawn and dusk were optimum, just after sunrise for a few hours and another couple of hours before sunset. Midday and the sun was too high, and likewise the wrong time of year and the sun wouldn't be in the right place either.

She couldn't make it rain, and she couldn't tell the sun when to shine, and she believed she'd never match the timings to the conditions.

There was one morning when Daisy, next door, stood alone in her dew-drenched garden, her elderly face upturned to catch the fresh morning rays, and Freya grabbed her opportunity. The sun was low and the air was misty. Freya spun in the sky and flung out her arms and screwed up her face in concentration.

The sun filtered through the pale mist and rested warm between Freya's fingers. The rays played around Freya before they reached Daisy's wrinkled skin and Daisy opened her eyes. The bright light played a trick on her before she blinked and turned away with blue/black spots dancing before her eyes. She glanced over the fence at her neighbour's garden and drank in the beautiful fragrance of the summer freesias and lavender, and she remembered watching Freya picking bunches of freesias with her mother just the year before.

Freya's image remained in her mind for much of that morning, but she missed the feint, very feint colours that had pervaded the morning dew.

Freya tried again just a few weeks later, this time for the Hillmans who lived a few streets away.

She watched the Hillmans a lot and her heart ached for old Thomas. His face betrayed his tortured emotions, but not a trace of pain or remorse was ever found when his beloved Joan turned her face to his.

The couple, both well into their eighties, were inseparable. Thomas had retired almost thirty years ago, and they had settled quickly into a comfortable and easy retirement. She was a seamstress, or had been at least until a few years ago, her embroideries and tapestries decorated the walls of their cosy home and patchwork quilts covered each bed. She had given up knitting and lace making when her fingers had become too painful with arthritis, but it was the embroidery that she refused to let go. She had a small hoop that sat on a velvet cushion in their living room, beside the white Persian cat. The piece of cloth held tight within it contained the image of another cat, and was at present half embroidered. Joan would spend just a few minutes each day threading the needle through the pattern, just a few stitches, but she refused to give up.

Thomas was just as stubborn; his vegetable patch was one to be envied.

There he was every day, hoeing, digging, weeding, planting and watering, and no one would have any idea of the pain that coursed through his frail body.

Disease riddled his body, and the only other person who knew was his doctor. Even Freya had no idea, but she knew something was wrong as she watched him watch his wife.

Thomas worried about his wife.

Freya worried about Thomas.

So she made him a rainbow.

He sat outside taking a well-deserved rest from an afternoon's hard labour. The shower earlier pleased him, because it meant he would no longer need to water the patch. His asters, chrysanthemums, coneflowers and rudbeckia all drank up the late afternoon's summer sun and he lazed contentedly in his dark-green deckchair. His eyes closed as the warmth danced across his skin, and he allowed himself a little nap. When he woke he saw what he thought was the last fading moments of a rainbow.

The palest red, orange, yellow, green, blue, indigo and violet tinged the sky before disappearing into the ether, and Freya's momentary, but most successful yet, rainbow brightened his day.

ELEVEN
WEARY

Freya wasn't the only one worried about old Thomas. Jen, from the Post office, remembered how he held his wife's hand at the funeral, and she noticed the sad and earnest looks he gave her when she wasn't watching. She saw how he'd reach for Joan's hand as they stood in the queue in the shop. There was a weary air to his gait and a solemn look in his eyes that only truly softened when he gazed at his wife.

But Jen didn't know what was wrong, and neither did Freya.

Freya didn't find out until her Mum took Jasmine for her Measles, Mumps and Rubella vaccination. She meant to stay with Jasmine and try to offer supernatural support but her attention was diverted when Thomas Hillman entered the surgery and sat down with a tired sigh.

Joan wasn't with him and that surprised Freya, who had seriously thought they were coupled by an invisible thread. Today that thread stretched as Joan went shopping and Freya accompanied Thomas into the doctor's room.

She didn't understand cancer, it was just a word that made people sad, but the pleading by the doctor, something unusual in itself, was enough to demonstrate the seriousness of what was wrong with Thomas. Freya reached into the vastness of her expanded mind and understood the depths of his disease.

Thomas still refused to allow his doctor to treat him. Hospital and clinic appointments were ignored, he only accepted prescriptions for stronger painkillers, and…his wife was not to know.

Freya sat in ghostly silence on the examination bed, allowing tears that would never actually drip onto the green-carpeted floor stream down her cheeks.

Jasmine's cry interrupted Freya's mind from the other side of the surgery, but her momentary pain was nothing to the pain, both physical and mental, that seeped through Thomas.

TWELVE
RECOGNITION

Freya became adept at reading expressions. She could not read thoughts, but her mind's growth had given her access to understanding psychology, which is what lead her to the Post Office.

Mrs French, the Post Mistress, momentarily glanced over at her daughter and wondered, for the tenth time that day, what she was thinking. For a few days now Jen had been preoccupied, but she hadn't shared her worries with her mother.

She smiled as Jen released a long, unconscious sigh and then shook her head, as if ridding herself of the webs of thought entrapping her mind. Jen sighed again and rubbed her eyes, it had been a long day and retiring upstairs for a long, hot bath would be just the thing she needed.

"Why don't you finish now," Mrs French said as if reading her daughter's wishes. "I've shut down over here, we're closing in half an hour, I'll finish everything off."

Jen stretched her arms up high above her head and yawned. She nodded and replied. "That would be lovely, thanks Mum, I'll return the favour."

Mrs French watched as her daughter disappeared and listened to her fading footsteps as she went upstairs.

Mrs French sighed. Jen hadn't had it easy, who does these days? But Jen really hadn't. It would be lovely if she could just find herself a nice, young man…but it was easier said than done. She smiled as she heard the hot water pipes start to clank and shudder. A hot bath would do her daughter good.

It had been a difficult few months for the whole community, something that up in her bath, Jen contemplated.

Jen was convinced something was wrong with old Mr Hillman, and it troubled her. There was a look in his eyes that she recognised but could not quite put her finger on…

Then she did.

Jen had lost her husband of seven years a few years ago herself. He'd had leukaemia, and had gone downhill very fast. It was quite treatable these days, but his strain, if that was the right word, had been aggressive and it was the look in his eyes that she now recalled. A stubborn look that told her he was fighting, but always behind his eyes there was pain, an expression that told her his fight would be futile. He would look at her tenderly and earnestly and his hand would reach for hers with an insistence she now understood only too well.

With a lump in her throat, she recognised the look that Thomas Hillman gave his beloved wife.

Freya saw the recognition and knew that finally someone other than Mr Hillman's doctor knew the truth.

THIRTEEN
SUNFLOWERS

"Why is everybody so sad?" Freya could hardly put her thoughts into words. "Down there, why are they all so sad?"

Freya sat beneath her willow with a small group of friends, and they watched as she wrung her hands. Ben spoke first. "Because they're not here?"

"Because we're not there anymore," said Keira pushing back her long, black curls. "They miss us!"

Ben sighed and Sophie curled her arm around his small shoulders.

"But we're happy up here." Freya's arms flew out as she encompassed her heaven. "This, all we've got here is amazing!"

"But they don't know that," said Carlos.

Freya slumped again. "…and we can't tell them…" She shook her head.

"Wouldn't make any difference if we could," said Carlos, shrugging his shoulders.

"It might help!" insisted Freya.

"How?" asked Abu, his dark, almost black eyes piercing Freya. "Telling them can't change anything."

"It might, I just want to let mum know I'm okay, I'm happy..." Freya's voice broke.

Carlos put his hand on her arm. "I know what you mean, but we'd still be gone, that wouldn't change."

Freya's lip wobbled. "I've broken their hearts, and there's nothing I can do to help."

A small voice piped up from the back of the group, and little Mai spoke softly in her oriental lilt. "It will pass, they'll understand..."

"But it's my fault, I did something stupid and now they're sad. I've wrecked everything!"

"They're just going through something terrible, but in time they'll learn from it," said Mai, "In time, they'll appreciate everything good so much more. We go through the bad to heighten the good." Mai got up and straightened her skirt then stepped lightly through the children and settled on the grass beside Freya. She looked up at her through thick, black lashes, her smile evident in her almond eyes, and spoke softly. "Freya, you're so new, you're still missing people, they're still missing you, it's still raw and it takes time for things to change, but I think there are a few things you haven't seen."

"What haven't I seen?"

Mai glanced about her and got a few nods in return. "I think we should show you a few things..."

As the little girl took Freya's hand she suddenly found herself back in Daisy's garden with Mai at her side. Daisy leaned against the fence with a wistful smile on her face. Next-door, Freya's mother stood on the grass watching Jasmine pull freesias from the flowerbed.

The stalks clasped in Jasmine's hands were squashed and widely varying in length, some of the lower buds were damaged and several stalks were broken, but none of that mattered. Jasmine continued pulling up yellow and purple and white freesias, and when her hands were full she stood up and grinned in delight.

Jasmine looked up at her mother and giggled. "Mine fowers," she said and without any hesitation she skipped over to the fence and offered the bunch to Daisy.

Daisy accepted the limp assortment with the same grace as if she'd just been offered an expensive bouquet of red roses. She held the flowers to her nose and inhaled. "Oooh, they are gorgeous!" she enthused and Freya could see the tears misting up Daisy's eyes.

"Your fowers." Jasmine beamed like a ray of sunshine.

Freya glanced from Daisy to her mother and Rachel pulled her cardigan sleeve over her hand to wipe away a stray tear too. These tears, however, were not of sadness but of gratitude and delight, as Jasmine made sure that Daisy would continue to receive her summer bouquets of beautifully fragrant freesias.

Freya smiled, and Mai tugged her arm. "That was because of you," she told Freya. "Now c'mon, there's more to see. We're going to school." Mai took Freya's hand.

Before Freya could question Mai she was in her old school's assembly hall. She couldn't help grinning as memories flooded back, and she followed Mai through the sea of red and grey.

The children all sat quiet and expectant all dressed neatly in a new term's uniform. Boys' trousers were smart and clean, no mud or holey knees, shoes were polished and unscuffed, and red sweatshirts were generally slightly too big or too small, as parents attempted to make them last an extra year or so.

Mai motioned for Freya to sit at the end of what would be her new year's row. Freya sank down, cross-legged, in the space between the last pupil and the teacher's sandaled feet. She glanced at the boy to her left, who was totally oblivious to his extra-terrestrial classmate. Giggling to herself, she leaned towards him and whispered his name in his ear. "William…"

He gave no reaction and Freya screwed up her nose and harrumphed. She looked up to her right, Mrs Atkins sat surveying her new Year Threes and a wry smile played on Freya's face, she would have enjoyed being part of Mrs Atkins' class. Mai settled delicately in front of her and told Freya to concentrate.

Freya looked up as Mr Buxton, the Head Teacher, rose and marched across the floor. "Good Morning, and welcome to a new school year." He rubbed his hands together and offered the pupils a big smile as they returned his greeting, with an enthusiastic harmonious. "Good morning Mr Buxton."

Freya tuned out as Mr Buxton's 'New school year' speeches bored her. She leaned forward and searched the row of children. There was Megan, halfway along listening intently to Mr Buxton. Freya stared keenly at her best friend, willing her to glance away from the Head, but Meg's attention was firm. Freya opened her eyes wide and concentrated hard on Meg, but it made no difference. Then she felt Mai jab her in the side. "Listen," whispered Mai.

Mr Buxton paused in his rhetoric and took a deep breath. "Now you all remember Freya Scott?" He paused to allow the murmured assents and nods, and Freya felt a shiver tingle from the tip of her scalp to her toes. Her attention was absolute. "She died in a tragic traffic accident during spring term earlier this year. We will be doing two things to commemorate young Freya…the first thing we will be doing is planting an apple tree in the school's wildlife patch, we will be planting the tree, which was most kindly donated by Heather's Nurseries, this afternoon. Mrs Atkins' Year Threes will be carrying this out just after afternoon registration." He paused again while the Year Threes whispered amongst themselves. He cleared his throat. "The second thing will be 'The Sunflower Award'."

Mr Buxton turned to Miss Allen, who had risen from her chair and held out a gold-plated sunflower atop a black, plastic plinth. He strolled across the hall and took the Sunflower from Freya's tearful Year Two teacher.

Back before the assembly he cleared his throat again and clicked his heels. "We conferred with Freya's family; after Miss Allen's old class asked if we could have something to remind them of their sadly missed classmate. Between us, we came up with this." He gestured to the award in his hands. "'The Sunflower Award'. Now, you all have different weekly awards in your classes, 'Pupil of the week' and suchlike, this will be for the whole school. Each month we will award it to the pupil who has made us the happiest. You will receive the Sunflower to adorn your classroom for the following month, and you will receive a certificate.

"How the pupil will be chosen was also discussed, and you will notice a yellow box in the foyer, by reception, any suggestions of pupils you feel deserve the award should be posted there, and myself and the teachers will discuss and make our own recommendations at the end of the month. We very much hope that the memory of Freya, a happy and cheerful little girl herself, will help the ethos of this school. We hope that you will remember our code…" Mr Buxton paused to allow the children to join in; the younger ones did with gusto, the older ones with more than a hint of embarrassment. "'*Help us to work, and never to shirk. Thoughtful and caring, loving and sharing. This message for all, will keep our school COOL.*'"

Freya giggled, along with many of the children, while Mr Buxton stood proudly, revelling in his achievements.

Mai smiled and nudged Freya. "Even your school motto makes people laugh!" she whispered. "Okay, let's go…"

The school faded around the two girls and Mai spoke again. "Are you seeing it now?"

"Seeing what exactly?"

"Joy, happiness? And *you* caused these things. You haven't wrecked anything! I can show you something else, something good that's only happened because of you."

A moment later and both girls were sitting on plumped up cushions, decorated with Van Gogh's sunflowers, across the room from two very different looking women.

The women looked polar opposites in every way, except the way they both held their steaming mugs. Both women must have insulated skin, either that or neither wanted to admit to scorched palms. Freya remembered her first mug of hot chocolate, some years ago. The mug had been so hot that despite her mother's warning so, she'd grasped the mug eagerly and then almost dropped it in searing surprise! In future she had always waited for the spiral of steam to vanish before gingerly taking her first sip, even if it meant that the drink was more on the cold side.

These ladies held their mugs close, with both hands wrapped around them, and sipped alike.

Freya smiled, she recognised the women. Mrs Taylor lived four, no, five doors up the road and Mrs Feldman lived next door, six doors up. It was well known that neither woman had spoken to each other for well over a decade.

Their husbands had had a feud over the boundary hedge, and it had grown, the hedge that was, to heights it had never known!

Mrs Feldman's husband had died first after cutting through his electric hedge-cutter's cable, on the very day he'd had enough of waiting for the Taylor's to the trim the hedge. After Mr Feldman's funeral, Mr Taylor had been consumed with remorse, devastated that his stubborn refusal to cut back the offending hedge had cost his neighbour his life. He had climbed up onto his wonky step-ladder, with his own pruning shears, and promptly slipped and broken his neck.

The two grieving women had not spoken since.

It was Donald and Daisy who had engineered the repair.

Donald had told Mrs Feldman that they would take her to the funeral and Daisy had offered a lift to Mrs Taylor.

The funeral, Freya's funeral, had touched their hearts and now they sat together, holding their mugs and laughing and gossiping as if they had been doing it all their lives.

"Life goes on," said Freya.

FOURTEEN
READY

"People find happiness, even when things are bad." Mai had been ready to stray from examples of happiness and contentment caused by Freya; she would have whisked her across the world showing her joy and delight. She was ready to share the wonder of gazing into a newborn's face, the first rains of a dry season, the first throes of romance, freshly picked strawberries, the lasting happiness of an elderly couple holding hands, ice-cream at the seaside, fish and chips in newspaper, singing, catching snowflakes, dancing in the rain, swinging as high as you can, rainbows...the list was endless.

She could do the same for despair and suffering, but it wouldn't be as much fun. Mai knew her point had been made, one couldn't exist without the other, and it was the same the whole world over.

Freya was thinking about freesias, and sunflowers and friendships, and, she smiled, Mr Hillman had all three.

Mai tugged Freya's arm and gone was the floral living room, instead the two girls stood amid bluebells considering Mai's illustrations.

"So," began Freya, "it doesn't matter what happens, happiness and sadness are all part of life. If I didn't know sadness, I would never know happiness. Mr Hillman is…how do I explain it? He knows how much pain is stored up, and he's just trying to, to give his wife more and more happy times, so when, when he's gone she'll have reserves of happiness to draw on." Freya paused. "Did I explain that right?"

Mai ran her hand through her silky, black hair and smiled at her. "I think you did."

Freya's soul danced and she grabbed Mai's hand, and they giggled and ran, zigzagging through the bluebells.

Jake and the other children joined them almost immediately and they collapsed in a riotous heap.

It was Mai who stopped giggling first, her eyes misted and her soul leapt and suddenly all was quiet. The jolt that struck the children could only be described as a flash of electricity flowing from mind to mind, and Freya, having never experienced the collective mind, reared back on her heels. "What's going on?" she asked.

Mai got to her feet with tears rolling down her shining face. Her lips curled into a serene smile and her whole being emanated joy.

Freya glanced from one child to another, and saw Mai's expression reciprocated in every countenance. "What's happening?"

Keira laughed gently and wiped a tear from her own eye. She scrambled up and threw herself at Mai. "I *just* knew you wouldn't be here long!" she cried into Mai's shoulder.

Mai continued to smile with a serenity Freya had never encountered before. Jake leaned close and whispered reverently. "Mai's ready."

"Ready?" asked Freya.

He nodded. "Ready."

"So soon?"

Mai turned to Freya. "Showing you today what you needed to see, confirmed what I already know." She reached up and embraced Freya. "I am ready."

"Then what are we waiting for!" squealed Keira, all reverence forgotten, "Let's go!"

Mai slipped her hand into Freya's and smiled. "Let's go."

The troupe followed the two girls and drifted across the springy grass. Mai moved purposefully towards Freya's orange blossom and aquilegia's. "This way," she said. They progressed through papery paeonies and bearded irises and as they moved through Freya's garden the planting altered. Freya didn't notice at first, but suddenly her wild, country flowers had smoothly transformed into delicate, oriental blossoms.

Pastel-pink camellias, surrounded by their dark leaves, overshadowed tiny orchids then the grass disappeared and gravel crunched beneath their feet. Ferns sprang up and moss blanketed the rocks that lead them past a gentle rivulet. More irises grew in the boggy grass beside the gravel path and magnolias spread their beautifully contorted branches, swathed with magnificent pink-blushed blooms, over their heads.

"Is this *your* garden?" whispered Freya in awe.

"Some of it." Mai nodded.

Tall bamboo rustled, and up ahead the grey shingle stretched out across the path, widening into a courtyard.

The noise of a waterfall reached their ears, but they could not see it, instead they saw a shallow pool lying ahead filled with huge water lilies. As they moved closer, turquoise and jade dragonflies flit to and fro, dipping down to the water and up again.

At the pool Mai turned to her friends and released Freya's hand. "From here I go alone," she told them.

They sank down to the gravel and leaned against the stone pool, and watched as Mai stepped away and moved off down the path. They could see again where the path widened, and an old gnarled wisteria stood in the centre of the garden up ahead.

Freya watched as Mai stepped lightly on. The little girl's gait changed from shy and nervous to assured and confident, and as it did, her ivory dress altered, just slightly, the skirt lengthened and lost the girly bounce it had always had, and its ivory changed to pure white.

A breeze caught Mai's hair and as the girl turned her head to smile and wave for the last time, all the watching children let out their breath. Mai's whole countenance changed, for a moment they saw a woman, young, slender and beautiful, turn and wave and then she was Mai again.

In that moment a figure had appeared, with outstretched arms, at the wisteria. Mai hesitated for a moment then ran into those welcoming arms. The light that infused the garden was blinding, and when the watching children had finished rubbing their eyes, the wisteria stood alone, gnarled and beautiful, but alone.

FIFTEEN
DIZZY

Nobody spoke as they wandered on. They had dashed to the wisteria, open-mouthed and awestruck, but it was just a tree, nothing more. They had circled it, run their hands across the twisted trunk, and stared into its contorted boughs, but Mai had gone.

Deep in thought they wandered on through the garden, finally coming across a small pagoda.

"This was Mai's favourite place," Sophie told them.

"She hardly spent any time here," said Keira.

Sophie smiled, fingering a piece of bright blue silk that whispered in the breeze. "She didn't need to."

Mai had decorated her small sanctuary with silken cushions and a turquoise Chinese rug. The whole effect was as if a peacock had chosen the décor himself. Deep green and blue voile hung from the ceiling and the tones were perfect set against the grey stone columns.

Sophie moved lightly up the two little steps and settled on the floor against a collection of cushions, she grabbed the nearest teal-blue pillow and hugged it to her chest. Keira followed and did the same. As the other children entered the pagoda and sat Keira sighed deeply and spoke wistfully. "When will *I* be ready?"

"As soon as you want to be," replied Abu, "I will be soon I hope."

"Carlos will be next," predicted Keira, prodding the boy's arm.

Carlos nodded. "It won't be long," he agreed.

Freya's eyebrows rose in surprise. "You know when you'll be ready?"

"I *am* ready, I'm just waiting."

"For what?"

"Not what, but who," he said with a smile. "Cholera's a terrible thing, my little brother's been and gone, my sister will be here soon, and then we'll go and join my parents."

"That's awful!" said Freya wringing her hands.

Carlos shook his head. "No it's not, it's better than where we were."

"That's the truth!" Abu grinned wryly.

"Were you from the same place?" asked Freya, confused.

"Do I look Mexican?" asked Abu.

Freya shook her head.

"We lived and died in similar circumstances, but on opposite sides of the world," said Abu.

"Cholera?"

"No, poverty."

"Poverty induced cholera in my case," said Carlos.

"*I* died of food poisoning, how ridiculous is that!" Keira joined in, her Irish accent thick with irritation. "Some idiot didn't prepare his food well enough and I died! I'm angry and my parents are as sure as hell angry!" She smiled apologetically. "It's gonna take me a while!"

"That's your problem," said Sophie ruefully. "Anger, like Abu's stubborn bitterness."

"It's not stubborn, it's justifiable...I'm missing a lot being dead, poverty or no poverty," Abu continued, "School was just around the corner, I could have gone in a few years, I could have been someone!"

"I'm not missing anything." Ben's voice was quiet, but had a hard edge. Sophie rubbed his shoulders. "My parents didn't want me and carried on as if I never existed...as you can see I didn't last long."

"We've all had it hard," said Jake.

Ben flinched and struggled for a moment to find his words. "*Not* in the same way... You had it alright *until* the day it went wrong, my life never began, never went right."

"Shush Ben, shhh," Sophie tried to soothe the young boy.

"My parents let me fend for myself..."

Jake paled, but was quiet, and Sophie hugged the small boy close again, as if her embrace could in some way make up for six years of neglect.

Freya shivered. Ben was always defensive, and Sophie always compensated, but looking at Ben now all Freya could see was a hurt and bewildered six-year-old. Freya had got used to seeing the children as older. Their speech was that of older children and the more time Freya spent immortal, the less ages were defined. They had turned into ambiguously ageless children, but their conversing had brought home to Freya just how young they really were.

Freya suddenly understood why they were there, why she was there, and knew that acceptance would be the first step in moving on.

She thought for a moment. "Ben had it right you know, most of us have had it good *until* it went wrong...I know some of us have had it really hard, but there must have been good moments, there must have been..."

Carlos smiled; his thoughts were centred on the imminent arrival of Inez, his baby sister. "I love her laughter, even now, cradled in Aunt Serena's arms, she laughs..."

For the second time Freya recognised the collective mind as they gazed down at a toddler resting in the tired arms of her aunt. Inez was pale and limp, but her face shone as she grinned.

"She'll be here soon," whispered Carlos, then he went on, "I love the blue sky, the warmth of the sun's early morning rays, rain on a hot day. I loved Aunt Serena's soothing voice…her safe arms when we were left alone, her love, her grace when all was lost."

As he spoke images from his memory emerged and rippled before them, then faded like echoes.

"I loved Mam's dinners," broke in Keira, "I loved her cooking, and I loved her soups…" She paused to relish the taste she could clearly remember, and the aromas she could smell in her mind. "Chicken, and leek and potato, and creamy tomato, ooh, I can taste them now, I *miss* them!" She laughed. "And I miss my Mam, I miss her so much…I want to sit at the table and watch her cook…"

Keira's mother was plump and aproned and stood beside a large old-fashioned aga, in an old-fashioned kitchen, all green and white gingham, and lacy, cottage curtains. She stirred the thick, steaming broth in the pan on the stove, and took in a deep breath of its aroma. Keira did the same inhaling through her nose with a huge exaggerated sniff.

"Oooh, leek and potato…" breathed Keira.

Three children sat at the huge wooden table, each grasping spoons with anticipation. Keira sat at the head of the table, her two older brothers banging the butt of their spoons on the table.

"Hush, and wait…" came her mother's voice from the kitchen.

"Aiden stop it!" reproved Keira with a frown. "Banging won't make it any quicker and you're giving me a headache!"

Aiden pounded his spoon louder and grinned widely. He dodged away as Keira's fist lashed out and he fell against his brother. He laughed loudly as Declan's spoon clattered to the floor.

Keira's mother turned from the stove with raised eyebrows and a wooden spoon at half-mast in her hand, it was enough to reduce the boys to smothered giggles. Keira regarded them with aloof superiority. "It'll be me that gets the soup then," she said, and the boys smoothed out their faces and sat in mock politeness for a moment, before dissolving into raucous guffaws.

Keira slipped off her chair and skipped into the kitchen. She reached up and grabbed a bowl from the surface and moved close to her mother. "Mammmy…" she wheedled, rubbing against her mother's skirts like a contented cat. She looked up and smiled as her mother dropped the spoon into the pan and caught her daughter up in her arms. Keira was in heaven, her mother's hug enveloped her and the aroma of home cooked soup filled her nostrils…

All the children in the pagoda breathed in simultaneously, and Keira sighed. "Oh, it was good!" she said. "I was wasted, dying of food poisoning…"

Abu conjured up his own vision, and a vision of colour it was! Red peppers, green peppers, onions, white rice, saffron coloured rice, turmeric and ginger, mango, mustard, cloves, green coriander leaves, dill, cumin, black pepper… He opened his eyes. "I didn't get to eat all that…" he said shaking his head, "But I imagined I could…one day"

Sophie stepped in. "I remember butterflies," she said softly. "I love butterflies."

Suddenly butterflies of all colours and designs fluttered around the gazebo. Sophie grabbed Ben's hand and pulled him to his feet. She jumped down the little steps, towing Ben with her. "Look!" she cried and threw her arms up in the air. She twirled and whirled, dancing with the myriad butterflies. She seized Ben's hands again and skipped in circles. Keira jumped to her feet and joined the circle grabbing Ben's hand on one side and Sophie's to the other.

Freya leaned out of the pagoda, resting her chin on her hands on the low wall. She glanced at Jake. "You haven't said much," she said.

He shook his head, but smiled as a butterfly landed on Freya's nose. She went cross-eyed and laughed. The butterfly lifted away and fluttered over Jake's head.

Carlos swung his legs down the steps and jumped up to join the dancers and Abu leaned forward to watch. The butterflies didn't stop, they fluttered and waltzed between the children, mesmerising Freya.

Memories were powerful, and good ones even more so.

Ben let go of the girls' hands, but continued revolving round and round, until he got dizzy. He wasn't really dizzy, it wasn't possible to be, his mind was strong enough to counter the motion, but Ben *was* dizzy and he was smiling, and he recalled the luxurious physical response to spinning on the spot…in an empty room, with walls of torn wall-paper, and a floor clothed in threadbare carpet, but Ben was happy as he spun.

Freya watched with tears in her eyes, as Sophie, Keira and Carlos slowed to a halt. They stood watching Ben, aware of the barely papered walls and floorboards between the scraps of carpet, and dirty, cracked ceiling. Aware of the mattress atop the dirty divan, and the thin blanket and the lone, rusted, matchbox car. Conscious of all these things, but also aware that Ben was happy, lost in his memory of a solitary moment when his painful childhood was eased.

SIXTEEN
SAGUARO

It was all Freya could do to stop herself tearing down the dusty road after Carlos.

Carlos was ready, he'd always been ready, and he knew the moment his baby sister arrived.

His shining face far surpassed serenity, and joy couldn't even touch it. He moved with the ease of tumbleweed and the grace of a light wind, and made his way down the dustbowl of a highway. Not much adorned the road, a patch of yellow desert marigolds bobbed atop their silver green foliage, and blue hyssop doggedly pushed through the wayside's dry earth, but aside from a giant saguaro towering in the distance and a few obligatory prickly pears, Carlos hadn't needed anything else.

Freya bit her lip, willing Carlos to turn around. She already knew he'd changed, his countenance had already matured, and even without the backward glance, she could see he walked with the assuredness of a young man.

The road was long, but Carlos remained steady and the sunset before him cast a lengthy shadow behind. It was just an illusion, Freya told herself, there were no shadows in heaven, and no suns either, but this was Carlos' illusion, his perfect moment, and the sun blazed in the azure sky.

Carlos became a dark figure against the sun, and the only thing to measure him against was the saguaro. The cactus stood, black before the sun, its upturned arms stretching towards the golden, cloudless sky.

Suddenly, ahead of Carlos, the saguaro was joined by a group of silhouettes.

A baby, a toddler, sat on the dusty floor, and Freya knew it was Inez who gazed down the road with adoration in her face. By her side was a small boy, just a little smaller than Carlos himself, who stretched out his arms to Carlos, and at the rear of the cluster, hands gripped tightly, waited a young couple.

A ripple of delight passed through the group of watching children, and Carlos picked up his feet to sprint into those waiting open arms.

The setting sun dipped a little lower, and a rose blush spread across the horizon, then the golden bronze sky brightened and pure light infused the atmosphere, and when it lessened, Carlos had vanished.

SEVENTEEN
DREAMS

Freya's thoughts returned to her family.

Jasmine stood at the top of the steps to the house. She clung tightly to the black post beside the steps and peered underneath the rail. She observed the huge man, mounting the steps, with trepidation. He was all in black, from top to bottom, and the big black, goldfish bowl covering his head was scary. She stared and clung even tighter. Then he reached both hands up and lifted the little window at the front of the goldfish bowl and showed his face.

Jasmine let out a little breath, and put on her bravest, most bold, face, as the hairy man climbed closer.

Uncle Pete pulled off a glove and stuck it under his arm then waved enthusiastically at the little girl staring at him with such solemnity. Her eyes filled with terror and tears and Uncle Pete caught on. He paused and raised his arms once more to twist and lift off his motorcycle helmet. As he did, the glove slipped from under his arm and flopped onto the ground. He bent to retrieve the glove and stuffed it into the helmet.

When he waved and smiled again, Jasmine looked somewhat calmer, but still unsure.

There was a loud squeal from behind the little girl and Uncle Pete's grin widened. He held out his arms as Jasmine's mum jumped down the steps and threw herself at her older brother. His leathers creaked and Rachel released him. "You could've shaved!" She grinned. "C'mon Jaz, say hello to Uncle Pete."

Jasmine remained on the steps, still clinging to the rail.

Uncle Pete raised his eyebrows and lowered to his knee. He watched Jasmine with a smile that Freya recognised.

Freya moved close to Jasmine and whispered in her ear. "Go on, he wants to give you a bear hug…"

Jasmine chewed her bottom lip and regarded Uncle Pete with suspicion.

The girls' mum stood waiting. "She's not usually this shy," she told her brother.

"Well, she hasn't seen me since the funeral, and she doesn't know me as well as Freya…" His words trailed off.

Freya moved down the steps and stood between Jasmine and Uncle Pete. When it appeared Jasmine was never going to budge from the top step, Freya diverted all her attention to her beloved uncle. He patiently crouched, balancing on one knee, waiting for his niece, with his motorbike helmet beside him, but he was not aware of the niece who already approached him.

Freya longed to throw herself into his big, strong arms. To be lifted high above his head and twirled…

Suddenly a force stronger than the wind ripped through her and caught her up in its vortex, and she was impelled into Uncle Pete's arms along with her little sister.

Uncle Pete took Jasmine in his arms, gently, but firmly, and hugged her.

Freya allowed herself to be enveloped in his hug for as long as her mind would allow the illusion. Then she gently withdrew, and sat with a lump in her throat, watching the bond that began to form between her uncle and sister.

Freya accompanied the trio indoors, but like Jasmine, lost interest when the chat became adult orientated. Jasmine spent the afternoon traipsing up and downstairs, bringing down her cuddly toys, one by one, for Uncle Pete's approval. The little girl was oblivious to the sadness that pervaded the room when she dropped Purple Ted into Pete's lap.

The ensuing silence was filled with small sobs from Rachel and toddler chatter from Jasmine.

Uncle Pete held his sister and offered what comfort he could, whilst nodding and smiling at Jasmine and all her furry offerings.

The melancholy didn't last too long, which Freya knew would be a relief to Uncle Pete, and soon the chat moved to the kitchen so Rachel could prepare dinner.

"Have you spoken to Anna?" asked Pete.

Rachel nodded. "You?"

"Emails," he told her, "it's easier."

"For men!" Rachel grinned as she sliced a carrot. "Here." She offered a piece to Jasmine. "Calls to Canada are free at the weekend," she said.

"And when am I free at the weekend?" he asked. "And how on earth do I know what the time is over there? I have no idea of the time difference!"

"What are your weekends filled with then?" she asked.

Pete glanced at her then laughed. "Not much actually."

Rachel looked up at him and stopped chopping the carrot. "You know," she began, "You're welcome to come over here, anytime, you don't have to sit alone in that big old house you know!"

"Big old house!" he scoffed, "That little matchbox of mine?"

She laughed and waved the knife. "Whatever, but you don't have to, you're not far away, come visit more." She reached for another carrot. "You know Jasmine would like to see you."

"See you," repeated Jasmine from the floor, her mouth full of carrot.

Uncle Pete leaned back against the sink. "I didn't want to get in your way."

"In our way?" Rachel raised her eyes to him.

"You know, after Freya."

Rachel sighed. "You'd not be in the way Pete, not ever."

"Then maybe I will," he said grabbing a pinch of grated cheese from the bowl.

"Hey!" she cried and slapped his hand, "Get off the dinner!" She put her knife down and moved to the fridge. "Oh no," she groaned.

"What's wrong?"

"I forgot to get more milk." She sighed. "I need cheese sauce for the fish pie, but I've only got enough milk for breakfast tomorrow…"

Pete was already half way across the room. "Not a problem!" he called back, "That's what the bike's for, little emergencies, especially if I get an invite to dinner! See you in a mo."

Freya was quick to follow.

Uncle Pete's big, shiny motorbike was, and always had been, a magnet to Freya. Though, try as she had, she'd never been allowed to do more than sit on the back for a short ride up the street and back, and she doubted the speedometer's needle had risen higher than five miles an hour.

Right now there was nothing and no one to stop her!

Pete grabbed his helmet and pulled it on, waved at Jasmine and donned his gloves. He ran down the steps two at a time, and jumped onto his bike. Once astride, keys in ignition, he kicked back the stand and rolled the bike off the pavement. The bike roared into action.

Freya whooped in delight as she leapt onto the bike. After a quick shoulder check, Pete was off, flipping down the visor as an afterthought.

Freya was fluid; she made believe her hands were gripping Pete's jacket buckles, and that the wind was coursing through her long hair, as the late autumn sun kissed her face.

It was only a few streets away that Pete pulled up onto the pavement and stopped. He took off his helmet, pushed his gloves inside and placed it on the seat. He yanked out the keys, felt for his wallet and strode towards the Post Office Shop.

The bell jangled as he pushed the door open wide, and his boots clapped on the old linoleum floor. His feet tapped all the way to the refrigerated shelves, but Pete wasn't self-conscious. He loved the way he looked, decked in his biker finery. Nothing intimidated Pete, except perhaps, the disapproving look Mrs French gave him as he almost toppled a magazine rack.

Pete reached out and picked up a litre bottle of milk, blue top of course, none of that green or red lid skinny stuff for Pete.

He swung round, brandishing the milk, and almost knocked out poor Mrs Taylor as she stood intent on the cereal display. Pete grunted, as he shimmied left to avoid her wire basket. Mrs Taylor squeaked something unintelligible and Pete had the grace to blush.

With the milk, he clip-clopped across the shop floor, trying to avoid the Post Mistress's gaze and plonked the bottle onto the counter by the till.

Jen grinned at him, having watched his clumsy exhibition, and scanned the milk. "That'll be eighty-six pence please," she said.

Pete fished out his wallet and plunged his fingers into the cash compartment, not finding what he wanted he began to tip the coins out onto the counter. Jen smiled patiently.

"Oh hello Mr Hillman," she said brightly.

Pete glanced up and smiled at the old man who placed his basket on the floor behind him. He noticed Jen's concerned expression as she spoke warmly to the man, and he used her inattentiveness to search his pockets.

"How are you Mr Hillman," she said.

"Very well thank you, a bit of pain with the wet weather but today is glorious and that always helps an old man," he said cheerily.

"And Joan, not with you today?"

"She's good, stuck with her embroidery, nearly finished this one, so I can't tear her away."

"Oh that's lovely, never been good with a needle myself," said Jen. "Can't even sew a button."

Pete listened, wondering whether to interrupt. He chose not to, but wondered why he was prolonging the inevitable.

"You should try it," said Mr Hillman, "she says it's very relaxing."

"Maybe I will." Jen turned her attention back to the milk. "Eighty-six pence?"

"Um, I thought one of these tens was a pound coin…" Pete reddened, "You don't take credit cards do you?"

Jen indicated a sign on the cash register.

"If I spend over a fiver…" Pete sighed, "Oh well, it'll be a box of chocs for Rachel and something for Jasmine then."

Mr Hillman put his hand on Pete's shoulder. "You Rachel's brother?" Pete nodded. "Don't worry about the money, a few pence won't kill me!" He winked at Jen, who gave him a strange look in return. "And get a chocolate bar for little Jasmine anyway, I'm paying."

"No, no it's okay…" began Pete.

"I insist. You wouldn't deprive an old man in his final innings a chance to help would you? I'm building up my celestial store!" Thomas winked at Jen again, ignoring her troubled expression.

Pete shrugged, but Mr Hillman went on. "It's so sad about little Freya, they've been through enough, but I'll help where I can, and if little Freya up there is watching, I'm sure she'll be ready to greet me, especially if I give her little sister chocolate!"

There would be nothing gained from arguing the point with Mr Hillman, so Pete grabbed a Milky Way and placed it beside his bottle. Mr Hillman added coins to Pete's ten pence pieces and Jen counted out the money. Mr Hillman refused the change putting it into the Lifeboat fund's battered moneybox instead. "There you go," he smiled, "and that's another one stored up there."

Pete caught Jen's distressed look and shrugged at her, she shook her head, but smiled.

"Thanks Mr Hillman," began Pete.

"Call me Thomas, please, time is too short for pleasantries…"

Jen sighed deeply as Pete picked up his milk and bar of chocolate, and nodded to them as he left the shop. "Thanks Thomas," he called back.

Pete stowed away the milk and paused for a moment looking back into the store, where Mr Hillman paid for his purchases and Jen smiled as she pushed back her hair. Pete smiled and picked up his helmet and climbed onto the bike.

The door jangled and Mr Hillman came out. Pete was ready to put on his helmet, but the grin that lit up Mr Hillman's face stopped him. Old Thomas placed his shopping bags by the window and rubbed his hands with glee at the sight of the bike. "Now there's a beauty," he said, "Haven't seen one of these close up for quite a while, always whizzing down the road these things."

From astride the motorcycle Pete smiled.

"And if young Jen sees me admiring this…she's worrying enough for both of us." He took a quick peek back at the store window and waved his hand dismissively. "I can look, can't I?"

Pete got off the bike to stand by Thomas. "That you can," he replied.

"It's big, all that fairing," said Thomas, "What's the engine?"

"It's a 1200. Did you ever have one?"

Thomas nodded. "But not like this, I've not been on a bike for thirty years, or more, but I did have one. A Triumph Bonneville 750, many years ago," he said with pride. "And its exhaust gleamed as much as yours!"

"I haven't got anything better to do with my spare time," laughed Pete.

"No woman then?"

Pete laughed again. "No, no woman, yet…"

"Got to find yourself the right one then, one that won't make you give this up!" He pointed at the bike.

"Not so easy though is it?"

"Oh, they are out there, my Joan didn't like the look of mine 'til I took her out on it!" Thomas chuckled. "Then there was no getting her off it!"

"Then I need a woman like your Joan," said Pete.

"She said it'd be the death of me, and I've survived the bike by more than thirty years!"

"And counting," said Pete.

Thomas looked wistful for a moment. "And counting," he agreed. "Do you know, there's nothing I'd like more than another go…"

Pete raised his eyebrows. "At what?"

"Bikes, motorbikes…" said Thomas.

"Don't you dare," came a voice from behind them.

They both turned like guilty children caught with their fingers in the biscuit tin. Jen stood, folded arms across her chest, in front of the shop door.

"Don't you go filling his head with silly dreams," she said staring pointedly at Pete. "And don't *you* go filling your head with them either, Thomas, they'll be the death of you."

Thomas shook his head and waved his hand again. "It's not these that'll kill me, I can assure you of that," he said firmly, "But don't you worry, my dear, no one's going to take me on the back of a motorcycle are they?" He cast a quick glance up at Pete, who smiled and climbed aboard his bike again. "Just let me hear you start it up then," he said to Pete.

Pete obliged, and twisted the handlebar to offer a thick, guttural growl. Mr Hillman chuckled again. "Off you go then," he said as Pete put on his helmet and gloves.

Pete backed up the bike and saluted Thomas and Jen, before charging off down the road.

Jen leaned down and picked up Mr Hillman's bags. He took them with a twinkle in his eye. "Nice lad, that one, and Jen, my dear, it's those *silly dreams* that keep us alive."

EIGHTEEN
SNOW

The first snow fell in November, and Freya watched helplessly as her father stepped out into the cold night air, and moved through the softly laying snow to his wife.

"Come inside," he whispered, his warm breath caressing her cold ear. He slipped off his jacket and placed it about her shoulders. "It's late."

She nodded and rubbed her nose with the back of her hand. "It is it's too late."

He glanced at her face. She stared blankly then raised her face to the falling flakes. He wasn't sure if her face was wet with tears or snow, but her eyes glistened and her nose was red.

"Rachel," he whispered.

She sniffed, and bit her lip. "It's too late," she repeated quietly, "too late for Freya."

"Rachel." Joe moved in front of his wife and put his arms around her.

"She won't see the snow, won't build another snowman, won't…" her voice cracked, "won't…"

"Rachel…" Joe couldn't speak.

"She's gone, it's her birthday next week. Eight, she'll be eight." Rachel looked into her husband's eyes. "I went through the shops last week looking for birthday presents…Presents she'll never have. I even put some in the trolley, had to put them back."

Joe met her eyes and tears blurred his own vision.

"Joe, I miss her, oh, I miss her so much!" Rachel grabbed hold of her husband and buried her face in his shoulder. "What can I do?"

Freya's mother wept, noiselessly, while the snow fell, until Joe, his heart as wrung out as hers, gently took her elbow and guided her back indoors.

Freya stood alone, in the garden, as the world rapidly turned white.

NINETEEN
PAPER SNOWFLAKES

Freya knew Megan missed her as she sat with her elbows in her hands at Megan's desk watching her best friend. Meg's tongue peeped out of the corner of her mouth as she concentrated on the pair of scissors and the folded circle of paper in her hand. Meg paused and stared blankly at the paper. She sighed with frustration then deliberately began to cut. The scissors moved this way and that, snipping and trimming, and when Meg was finished she dropped the scissors and eagerly opened the circle.

Meg's sigh and grunt betrayed her disappointment as she held the freshly cut snowflake in front of her. "Oh, that's beautiful," said Mrs Atkins cheerfully.

"Mmm," mumbled Meg, "s'okay, but it's meant to have hearts all over it."

"What was that sweetheart?" asked Mrs Atkins.

"It's meant to have hearts in it, Freya could do hearts, she knew how to make hearts in the paper."

"And stars," said Steph leaning across the table, "she could do stars too."

"That's nice," said Mrs Atkins as she moved on and pasted a bright smile on her face before she picked up William's 'cut to bits' snowflake. "William, this is lovely!"

Both girls screwed up their faces and giggled. *"William, this is lovely!"* they mimicked as Mrs Atkins moved swiftly to the other side of the classroom.

William threw them a sour look and began to fold a new circle, when they didn't stop laughing, he picked up the scissors and brandished them at Meg. She squealed and Mrs Atkins was back at their table in no time.

"Come on girls, I want lots of snowflakes for the windows and you can choose your favourites to decorate your Christmas cards."

"I'm going to do small ones for my card," said Steph picking up a handful of pastel coloured circles, half the size of the ones Mrs Atkins wanted for her room decoration.

"Me too." Meg agreed.

Freya watched as Meg began again thinking deeply about the pattern as she cut. Again Meg released a disappointed sound and let the snowflake drop from her fingers.

"I wish Freya was here, she could do this!"

Freya herself, was there and wished she could help, but her fingers just slid through the scissors and there was nothing she could do.

She had watched Megan over the past few months. Meg had suffered the loss of her best friend with such anguish that her mother had not known how to deal with it. There aren't many textbooks on 'How to perk up your child when their best friend dies in a car accident', and Mrs Frost had decided to take the approach one might take if a family pet passed away. It was easy to cajole and distract, and a few carefully chosen school friends had been invited over to tea, one by one, as if Meg would suddenly nod and choose one to be her new best buddy.

Meg had not nodded, but had pulled so far away, that her friends had done the same.

Returning to school in September had been fine for Meg; she was desperate to escape her mother's worried looks and anxious hugs. Mrs Atkins was much more sensible, and ignored Mrs Frost's pleas for special treatment. Instead she placed Meg at the same table as Stephanie and let them get on with it.

Steph had risen to the occasion and allowed Meg precious space to breathe.

Right now, Meg watched as Steph expertly cut her snowflake. "Can you do hearts too?" she asked her.

Steph paused then nodded. "Freya showed me how to do them," she told her, "and stars too."

"And stars," murmured Meg in admiration. "She showed me too, but I just can't remember how."

Steph put down her small snowflake and picked up a larger circle, she folded it in half, then a quarter, then once more. "Look," she said leaning across the table to Meg. "Start here, you're starting too far up, you run out of space before you can make it…start here, and cut in diagonally." She moved her scissors deftly. "Then cut round at the top, but down a bit too, look…"

Meg slid closer over the table and watched as Steph rounded the top of the shape on the outside edge. Steph let the scissors slip out of her hands and unfolded the paper. "Look," she said and there sat a little heart, cut intricately into the white paper.

Meg smiled. "It's as good as Freya's."

"You try it." Steph refolded the paper and handed it to Meg.

Meg sighed deeply and flourished the scissors. "Like this?" She cut into the paper, and paused, Steph nodded and Meg's tongue escaped her lips again as she fed the folded paper through her fingers. "And round? And like this?"

When she finished she unfolded the snowflake with a worried expression, which dissolved into delight as the second heart shape stared at her from the snowflake.

"And stars?" said Meg hopefully.

"And stars." Steph grinned.

Freya sighed wistfully as the two girls concentrated on the Christmas snowflakes, and smiled to herself as the pile of fringed, heart and star filled flakes began to grow.

Mrs Atkins completed her circuit yet again, and stopped as she approached the table. She smiled to herself with the satisfaction of one who'd scored the winning goal, and lavished the girls in praise. "You have certainly got the best and biggest pile, this will really help us to win the best decorated classroom!" she told them. "Have you chosen the ones you want for your cards, or are you making more?"

"Making more Miss," said Steph, reaching back into the stack of paper Mrs Atkins had just replenished.

"I look forward to seeing them, these are the cards for your Mums and Dads," she told them.

Steph nodded. "I'm making blue ones, different blues…"

Meg sucked her lip between her teeth as she chose, but picked up pastel green, blue and pink. They began folding, cutting and snipping in earnest.

Steph finished first and jumped down from the table to get folded card to mount the paper snowflakes. "What colour do you want?" she asked Meg.

"White, like snow," said Meg.

When Steph returned they got stuck in and soon had two Christmas cards ready and waiting. They stood up their cards and grinned at each other.

"You're too fast!" groaned William, "I'm never gonna finish, my Mum will get a card with a blizzard…no snowflakes, just white paper!"

The girls laughed then Steph glanced surreptitiously at Meg. "What are you thinking?" she asked.

Meg twirled her finger in her hair, and leaned across to pick up a glittery circle of lilac. She smiled thoughtfully. "Freya would've chosen this."

Steph nodded. "She would."

"Are you thinking what I'm thinking?" asked Meg, her eyes shining.

"I might be," replied Steph with a half-smile playing on her lips.

Meg leaned conspiratorially toward Steph. "What about making one…"

"For Freya," concluded Steph.

Meg nodded and Freya grinned.

"We could make one for her Mum and Dad," said Steph, "because she can't."

Freya shivered; she had already picked out the colours she would have chosen as they had amassed their stack of decorations, for a moment she wondered if they'd read her mind.

Meg lowered her face. "Wouldn't they be upset?"

"I don't think so," said Steph, "C'mon, let's."

Between them Meg and Steph chose three paper circles; lilac, blue, like Daddy's t-shirt, and pale, shiny gold, like the stars on Freya's white dress. They snipped until they had three intricately cut snowflakes then they mounted them on pale blue card, and stood Freya's Christmas card up in front of their own.

"Freya would've made that!" Meg smiled and Steph nodded, and Freya tried to understand the twinge of both jealousy and gratitude.

Later, at the end of term, Meg and Steph emerged from school together, clutching bags of Christmas decorations and projects. Steph pulled her mother across the playground toward Meg.

Mrs Frost stood with a snowflake card in her hand and an apprehensive look in her eyes. "I'm not sure…" she said as Meg stared up at her, her eyes full of reproach.

Steph's mum strolled up with a huge smile and asked. "Let's see this wonderful card then."

Mrs Frost let it slip from her fingers and Steph passed it to her Mum, who enthused without reservation. "Oh it's beautiful, so lovely girls, so when will we deliver it then?"

Mrs Frost's expression altered from apprehension to unease, and Meg shot a gloomy look at Steph. Steph grinned as her mother winked at her and addressed Mrs Frost. "Can Meg come over for dinner tonight, I'll drop her back with you by seven?"

Meg pulled on her mother's arm and Mrs Frost relented seeing a quick way out of the awkward visit she had envisioned. "Tonight? Of course she can, seven is fine."

Meg and Steph grabbed each other's hands as their Mums swapped phone numbers and addresses, then whooped in delight once Mrs Frost was safely back in her car.

The 'awkward visit' was anything but. Freya's Mum opened the door with Jasmine on her hip. She looked tired and emotional, but she smiled as the cheerful woman on the doorstep introduced herself.

"Hi, I'm Olivia Turner, Steph's mum, and the girls have something very special they'd like to share with you…"

Freya watched that cold, winter day as the Christmas card she should have made took pride of place on the mantelpiece, and two very special friendships began.

TWENTY
SQUASHED SNOWDROPS

It felt quite bizarre to Freya to watch Meg visit more often than she had when Freya was alive, when Meg had been her best friend!

Mrs Frost, however, was over the moon that Meg had acquired a new friend and was doing her best to support it, even if that meant allowing Steph over for tea once in a blue moon. She was relieved though, that both Meg and Steph preferred disappearing with Olivia, Steph's mum.

Where Mrs Frost disapproved of the colourful Olivia, Rachel relished the friendship that had developed since she turned up on her doorstep with two nervous little girls and paper snowflakes.

There had been no more snow that year, except the flakes on the Christmas card and it now stood beside the lacy, purple and red heart valentine that the two girls had made for Rachel. "They want to make you the cards that Freya would have, just for a year." Olivia had confided in Freya's mum. "They don't want you to feel left out, but it'll only be for a year, though they'll probably forget about it after Easter. Is that before or after Mother's day this year?"

Rachel had shrugged and shaken her head with a smile. The cards were lovely and she really appreciated the sentiment, but she wasn't sure how easy it would be to accept a Mother's day card, when the time came...

At first Rachel wasn't sure about making new friends, she had become much more introverted since her daughter's death, and Olivia had looked like she might just be too much hard work, but Olivia wasn't to be deterred, and she made it her business to visit frequently, and more often than not, she would bring along both Steph and Meg. This delighted Jasmine who missed Freya, and still wondered out loud when she would come home.

So while her first visits were tolerated, Rachel soon came to look forward to Olivia Turner turning up.

It was Steph who, when Jasmine was plucking snowdrops out of the earth, helped her to dig up a baby hellebore instead to give to Daisy next door. Jasmine left a trail of squashed snowdrops en route to Daisy's back door, accompanied by Steph and Meg.

"For Daiseee," said Jasmine, clutching a muddy brown pot to her chest, as they knocked on the door.

Steph and Meg stood behind her. The door opened and Daisy smiled. "Hello girls," she said. "And what can I do for you?"

"More fowers," said Jasmine, "The uvver ones broked." Jasmine cast her eyes behind her to the snowdrop trail, and offered up the pot.

"So Jasmine's Mum said we could give you a baby hellebore," Steph told her, "There are lots more baby plants all round it!"

Daisy grinned, amused by the fate of the poor snowdrops. "Well Donald will be very pleased," she said, "he's always liked that hellebore, beautiful snowy white, and look at those flecks..." She pointed behind them at the parent plant. "Be a few years before this one's as good as that, but it's good to be patient."

Steph was trying to stifle a giggle. Daisy raised an eyebrow, and Meg nudged Steph.

"If you wait for a moment, I think I might have something in return." Daisy turned away and stepped back into the house. Jasmine followed without a thought.

Steph nudged Meg back. "Have they got a dog…called Pluto?" She erupted into giggles.

"Shut up," said Meg, "That would be Mickey Mouse anyway."

Jasmine emerged a minute later and ran her hand across the back door as she climbed down the step. Her muddy fingers left a smudge, but Daisy smiled. "Donald's got something," she told them and called behind her, "Donald…"

There came a strange shuffling sound and a white feather flew out of the door, quickly followed by another. The two older girls looked astonished and Steph stopped giggling. "Quack…quack," Another shuffle and a handful of feathers. "Quaaack, quaaack, quack!" And out of the door came Donald, his red face beaming and his snow-white hair greased into a quiff atop his head. "What did you expect? Donald Duck?"

Meg looked embarrassed, but Steph creased up, her guffaws bellowing across the garden. She laughed and laughed, and Donald and Daisy joined in. Jasmine smiled with that smile young children give adults when their humour soars right over their heads, and Meg smiled, when she realised no one was really annoyed at Steph.

"Oh, that was sooo funny!" Steph wiped her eyes.

"Donad duck?" said Jasmine, which caused everyone to burst out laughing again. "Is Donad a duck?" she asked.

"No sweetheart." Daisy smiled, "He's just pretending, and he'll do it again in a few years when you're a little older, just as he did for Freya!"

Donald went back inside and came out with feathers. "For me?" asked Jasmine.

"If you want one," said Donald, "But you might prefer one of these instead."

Jasmine nodded vigorously when he brought his other hand round from behind his back. He offered each girl a Twix, which they gratefully accepted.

"In return for the lovely plant," he said with a twinkle in his eye, "I've wanted one of those for ages."

Donald was still wearing comfy slippers as he stepped out into the yard, he moved across the patio and placed the pot with a small group of over-wintering plants, and then rubbed his hands together. "When the sun shines I'll plant these up," he told them, "Now for the feathers…"

The girls polished off their chocolate bars and watched with rising amusement as Donald began to chase white feathers around the backyard. Daisy collected their wrappers and Steph and Meg both bent to catch a stray feather that floated their way.

"Me help!" cried Jasmine and she bounded after another feather.

Daisy laughed as she stood in the doorway watching her husband and three little girls chasing feathers that whirled and danced around the yard. "You'll never catch them!" she chuckled.

"Got one!" shouted Steph and punched her hand in the air to wave her white trophy. Daisy nodded and Steph presented it to her then raced off after another.

The wind played havoc, lifting the feathers and dropping them, and spinning them and spiralling them around the girls' legs, happy with every squeal as a feather evaded the hand that grabbed at it. Hair flew about their faces and whipped up a little vortex in the centre of the patio. The delighted players converged and a rugby scrum formed as they created a barrier to keep the wind out.

Little hands snatched and they began to gather up the rogue feathers.

They'd collected most of them when the wind turned bitter and moments later the remaining white feathers were joined by huge, fat snowflakes.

The girls' screamed with glee and the feathers were forgotten as they lifted their red faces up toward the sky.

Donald cradled an armful of feathers and took them inside then he stood by the door with his wife. "Little Freya should be among them now," he said with a wry smile.

She nodded, both unaware of the unseen figure twirling alongside Jasmine, Meg and Steph.

Freya danced and frolicked in the snowfall, and dressed in white, decorated with a million tiny, silver snowflakes, and fur-lined, white boots, she was a sight they could not behold.

She moved as gracefully and as invisible as the wind, but she was there, dancing her heart out, face tilted trying to absorb the flakes that fell around her.

"I love snow!" shouted Steph.

"And me!" added Jasmine.

The three girls grabbed hands and began to dance in a circle. The snow began to lay and a circle of footprints emerged.

"Oh, would you look at them!" Olivia and Rachel appeared at the wall, summoned by the raucous noise, and gazed over into the yard.

"Mummy!" called Jasmine, "Look at me!"

Rachel nodded and grinned at the sight before her.

"Mummy," Jasmine shouted again, "get Feya, it snowing!"

Rachel's smile did not falter, but Olivia squeezed her shoulder.

Daisy and Donald shared a glance and sent a sympathetic smile across the wall.

"Mummy!" Jasmine jumped, delighted in the footprints she left, and she jumped again making her way towards the wall. "Mummy, look…feetpint."

Olivia lifted her hands and gave a quick clap. "C'mon girls, you're messing up the beautiful snow in the yard, come over this side and leave some fresh 'feetprints' over here!"

Jasmine rushed to say goodbye to her neighbours then jumped all the way to her own back door, with Steph and Meg following her little footprints.

They continued to enjoy the snow until their noses were red and cold and their fingers likewise, and then Olivia called them in to enjoy mugs of hot chocolate and biscuits.

Outside, Freya danced alone unaware of the cold, or the slush and squashed snowdrops at her feet.

TWENTY-ONE
FROZEN

Snow was just the beginning of a very cold snap, and Freya felt it on both sides of the veil.

Jake had become a different person to the one who had welcomed Freya almost a year ago, and she hadn't helped, despite the fact that helping was exactly what she was trying to do.

Freya floated down to the oval swimming pool. A huge, plastic sheet covered the pool, and an expanse of ice covered the blue plastic. That hadn't, however, deterred Jake's mother, who sat silent and cross-legged on a white, plastic recliner. Freya took the spare seat and adopted the same position opposite the icy lady. Jake's mother lifted her head and stared, sightlessly, into Freya's eyes.

There they sat and neither moved.

The piercing wind howled around them and Freya wondered what to do.

Moments later a door opened a few metres away from them and out stepped a middle-aged man. He sucked his breath through pursed lips and shivered, stepping quickly back into the house. He emerged a minute later, this time clad in a thick coat. He flapped his arms for a moment, smacking his thighs, then shook his head, stamped his feet and reached into his pocket. He pulled out a cigarette and lighter, and stuck the cigarette between his lips. He attempted to light it, struggling in the fierce gale, and bent to protect himself from the blustery weather.

For the first time Freya saw life surge into the ghostly woman, as she unhooked her legs and slipped off the lounger. She tiptoed across the icy terrace and moved beside the man. Her dress flapped against her bare legs and her hair blew wildly, and Freya watched as Jake's mother wrapped herself around the man.

He lit his cigarette and sucked fiercely, then held it in his fingers and blew out the smoke. The smoke was whipped away and he took another long drag. Her long, mousy hair coiled around his arm and stroked his face, and she moulded her body to his, longingly. Her dress wrapped itself around his leg and she hid her face in his camelhair coat. He stomped his feet to stay warm and lifted the cigarette to his mouth again. This time the wind swept around the house so violently he shook his head and stubbed out the cigarette on the brick wall. He shook his shoulders and clapped his hands, and shivered. Then he bent his head and blew into his freezing hands, turned and reached for the door handle.

The ghost, draped over his large frame, shivered and released him as he stepped back into his warm, centrally heated home, and Freya watched her crumble as he closed the door with a definite slam.

Jake's Mum remained prostrate beside the door, her dress still flapping in the storm.

Freya jumped off the plastic sun-lounger and ran to the house. She knelt beside Jake's mother and put her arms around the woman's shoulders.

The woman did not move, but slowly raised her face to meet Freya's. Freya did not cry, but she felt the memory of tears sting her eyes, and she lifted her hand to touch the woman's face. As she did Jake's Mum touched Freya's wrist and Freya felt the impression she left there. The woman stood and stepped away from Freya, their eyes still locked together, then she turned and ran.

She moved gracefully across the ice and threw herself into the billowing wind. Freya watched as the figure spiralled into the air and disappeared.

Later, Freya took Jake's hand and wrapped it around her wrist, pressing hard. Tears filled his eyes and he moved Freya's hand to his face. He brushed the back of her hand across his cheek, allowing the fleeting impression to touch him, and then let go. Freya watched as he too, disappeared into the ether.

TWENTY-TWO
RAIN

"Is that her?" Freya whispered and prodded Jake.

Jake nodded. "Quiet," he hissed.

"She's about to die?" Freya nudged him again.

"You know she is," he replied with a trace of reproach.

"Is this what it was like with me?"

"Will you stop asking questions? I didn't ask loads of questions, I just watched."

"But I haven't done this before," said Freya.

"Nor had I!" He frowned at her. "Now be quiet you're ruining everything."

Freya stared back down, suitably chastened. She had never witnessed such a scene before and an awkward sadness consumed her.

"I won't know what to say," she murmured.

Jake ignored her.

"How many of you watched my death?" she asked.

"Just myself and Mai," he replied without looking at her.

"Mai?"

"Mai."

"But she was younger than you."

"How many times do I have to tell you age has nothing to do with it?" He shook his head. "We just watched we didn't *talk*."

Below them, a small girl lay in her mother's arms, both propped up on pillows. Mousy hair sprouted from her head in little tufts, and her father gripped her limp hand whilst trying to avoid the coiling tube that emerged from the back of it. Two older girls sat, one hugging her father and wiping silent tears away, and the other motionless beside her, her hands clasped in her lap.

Freya stopped talking as the gravity of the moment suddenly hit her.

A curly-haired nurse stared absently out of the window, a doctor beside her, rubbing the clip of his biro softly with his thumb as he waited.

A murmur came from the small girl's pale, dry lips, but it was incomprehensible. Her mother rocked and tightened her hold on her dying daughter, and made no effort to check the tears that rolled down her face.

Freya leaned forward and tumbled away from Jake. Moments later she stood in the girl's room with only the sound of rain drumming on the windowpane behind her. She couldn't move, couldn't pull herself away, and couldn't take her eyes off the small girl.

The girl's chest barely moved, and the doctor stepped closer to gently touch her pulse.

Moments later the doctor shook his head, just the tiniest of shakes, and her mother drew in a deep and painful breath. Her silent sobs found voice and her shoulders shook as she hugged her child to her bosom. Her father released his little daughter's hand and took her siblings' hands, one in each of his, and he held them to his heart. Her sisters allowed their tears to fall as unrestrained as the rain sliding down the window.

The clouds outside were grey and heavy, matching the grief in the room, but Freya knew it was she, and she alone, who could see primrose rays making their way across the violet sky towards them.

Rays of celestial light broke through the windows and bathed the family in gold. The transcendental glory that surged through Freya was at odds with the grief surrounding her, but though she couldn't see inside the light she knew what it beheld.

Her soul yearned to reach out to the small, devastated family, but she knew that was not her job.

The light withdrew and Freya closed her eyes. For a single instant she saw the young girl, immersed by light, move and glide from her family, and then she was gone.

Freya could not stay, she was drawn away as the light faded and found herself back beneath the willow with Jake.

Neither spoke, it seemed wrong to do so, until, some while later, Jake whispered in her ear. "Go to her."

No explanation was necessary, Freya just allowed the thought to cross her mind and she was standing at the periphery of her garden. She looked around and before her was a landscape of soft, rolling clouds. In the centre of the clouds was a shaft of light, the same light that had shone and lifted her away from mortality, but as Freya observed, it diffused and vanished.

Freya stood at her boundary, wondering what her next move should be, when her legs decided for her and stepped onto the cloud.

It yielded to her step, but she did not fall through and she gently walked across the springy bank of cloud. She smiled as thoughts of candyfloss fluttered through her mind, and she just about managed to resist bending down to taste the huge, creamy-white mounds.

The clouds around her were bright and clean, as if they'd been washed and hung out to dry, but as she moved on they began to turn grey and foreboding. The clouds began to seethe and simmer, and Freya stepped carefully, feeling unsure of her footing. The blue sky darkened and turned violet, and spray flew up and around her as if she were walking on surf-tormented waves. The gloom spread and there beneath the stormy sky, sitting on top of a violent, purple rain cloud was Alice.

The clouds groaned and moaned, and Alice sat cross-legged, staring out across the vista with an expression as furious as the storm with which she was surrounded.

Freya stood taking in the incredulous scene, it was not one she ever imagined seeing. "Aren't you happy?" she asked, her voice barely audible above the cacophony.

"Do I look happy?" replied Alice.

Freya didn't want to state the obvious so she kept quiet. Instead she cast her eyes around and shook her head. Alice's cloud wasn't just raining; it was producing a full-blown waterfall…

"I don't want to be here."

"I can see that!" said Freya.

"They've just dumped me here," said Alice full of antagonism as mist rose around her.

"Not really dumped…" began Freya.

"And what kind of place is this anyway?" Alice spread out her arms to take in her clouds.

"What you make it," Freya muttered.

"I was going to beat it!" said Alice resentfully. "Mum said I could beat it! So I didn't want to die! I was going to make it…"

"But you didn't and here you are." Freya felt that it wasn't worth beating around the bush.

"But I don't want to be!" cried Alice.

"So you're going to sit on a cloud and make rain?"

"Isn't that what we're supposed to do? Sit on a cloud and grow wings?" replied Alice with contempt.

"I wanted wings," said Freya.

Alice ignored her. She raised her hand and threw a bolt of lightning.

"So you're just going to throw a tantrum then?" asked Freya.

"Well, aren't you Little Miss Self-righteous? It's okay, I've had the pep talk, you know." Alice threw her a look that was as thunderous as the clamour going on beneath them in the clouds.

For a moment Freya was at a loss. She stood and watched then moved closer and sat down beside the angry little girl.

"I'm not going to be full of radiant glory…" began Alice, "just radiation glory. My body went bad, and I've spent a year, a whole year, fighting it. It was never going to be roses and bunny rabbits when I finally got here."

"But you are here," said Freya firmly, "And how you deal with it *is* up to you."

"What's it to you anyway?" asked Alice glancing sideways at Freya.

Freya shrugged. "I'm here to help you through it, to help you adjust…"

Alice harrumphed.

"We've all been through it, but it doesn't have to be this hard," Freya continued. "You don't have to sit on stormy clouds."

"I want to sit on stormy clouds," Alice persisted, "If I can't go back, and they said I can't, I'd rather sit and sulk about it."

Freya shrugged again. "That's up to you, but it doesn't have to be this way."

"Are you staying then?" asked Alice.

"If you want me to."

"I haven't been on my own for a long time." Alice wiped away a tear, or it could have been a raindrop. "I don't want to be on my own."

"That's why I'm here." Freya reached out her hand, but Alice did nothing more than cast an annoyed look at it. Freya pulled it back. "You could have anything here, you know, you could have a real…wonderland."

Alice's face whipped up towards Freya. "Like I haven't heard *that* one before!" she spat.

"Sorry, I'm just trying." Freya kept her face expressionless.

Alice offered a watery smile. "Mum called me her little Alice in Wonderland."

The storm quelled and the dark clouds lightened. Alice began to cry, but this time the shower that left the clouds was just that, a shower. Freya extended her hand once again, and Alice moved closer, she allowed Freya to hug her, and the clouds slowly, very slowly, reverted back to a heavenly soufflé.

TWENTY-THREE
WONDERLAND

Alice kept her clouds. She'd spent so much time staring up at them through windows over the last year, she felt extraordinarily comfortable living on them.

"I wanted to die in my own bed," she reflected, "but I think that scared Mum, you know, having me die where they all lived… she got her way with the hospice. Dad wanted me home too, but I heard them one night, she couldn't bear the memories tainted with death if she had to keep on living there. I don't blame her."

"But you said you were going to make it," said Freya.

Alice shrugged. "Yeah, I was, but there comes a moment, when everyone knows it won't happen."

"What was it like, knowing you were going to die?" Freya couldn't disguise her curiosity.

Alice thought. "I was scared, at first, who wouldn't be? Didn't know what would happen, how it would happen, but they prepare you."

"How?"

"Read you stories, talk about theories, they talk about going to sleep. Mum said I'd go home to the angels." She grinned, "And here you are!"

Freya smiled. "I didn't know I was going to die, it just happened, I got run over."

"Is it harder knowing, or not knowing?" pondered Alice.

"I didn't get to say goodbye, I was just gone."

"We said lots of goodbyes. I'm still not sure if that's worse or not."

Freya shook her head. "I didn't get the chance to think about it, so it wasn't scary. I didn't have to wonder what it would be like."

"It's not what I thought it would be like," confided Alice. "I thought Granddad would be here to welcome me, not that I don't like you, but you never gave me sweets and hugs and *you* didn't teach me how to make 'crispie cakes'. It's not what I expected."

"That's because you're not ready yet," Freya told her with a conspiratorial smile.

"Ready? I've been ready for weeks!"

"Not that kind of 'ready', not ready to die, but ready to live!"

"Live?"

"To go on…"

"Where?"

"I don't know, but I bet your Granddad will be there to greet you and hug you!" Freya assured her.

"When does that happen then?"

Freya shrugged. "When you're ready."

They sat in contemplative silence for a while.

"I'm not ready yet," said Freya.

"Why not?"

"I don't know, we've discussed it a lot, and some people aren't ready because they're waiting for someone, some can't let go of the life they've left, or the people they've left." She paused. "I think, I can't let go of my family yet, it still makes me sad, I miss them…"

"You'll always miss them," said Alice.

"I know, but I watch my Mum, and...she cries, she still cries, and so does Dad. Mum doesn't know that Dad still cries for me. He won't wear his favourite blue t-shirt, it makes him cry. Mum found it the other day, folded up underneath his pillow. She left it there."

"My Mum doesn't like my rabbit," Alice shared. "It's a white one, you'd never have guessed!" Freya laughed. "She doesn't like him, my sisters' don't want him either, but Dad won't let her get rid of him. He said, 'Rabbits don't last long,' and Mum said, 'Nor did Alice,' but he won't let her get rid of him."

"Mum won't change my bedroom either," said Freya, "it's almost a year, but she won't do it."

"Mine's changed already. They took the hospital bed back."

"What did you think of your funeral?" asked Freya.

Alice chewed her lip. "It was nice," she began, "I'd rather have been buried...it'll take me forever to collect up all those little pieces of dust!" she joked. "Actually, I liked being cremated, which were you?"

"Buried."

"Oh, I was going to ask about the scattering, but you wouldn't know."

"Know what?"

"Does everyone 'feel' it?"

"What do you mean?"

"I, I mean, my ashes, were scattered across a stream, near where we lived, we used to play there when I was better. I 'felt' it," she said. "Dad shook the urn and out I came, for a moment I felt the wind caress me. I felt the breeze lift me and let me go...but I was up here, watching."

"It's memories..." Freya told her, "Your mind lets you feel what you can see. Up here, you've brought all your memories and experiences, and you can draw on them anytime!"

"And more!" exclaimed Alice, "It's amazing how much more I know!"

Freya smiled. "Have you been back?"

Alice nodded. "Yes, but I think it's too soon, still too much grief."

Freya sighed. "That doesn't change."

"Oh, it will, life goes on," said Alice. "Life goes on for all of us, just in different places."

"Hmmm, you're going to be ready sooner than I am!" Freya laughed.

"We'll see."

They both sat on Alice's fluffy, white clouds. "Are you going to change these?" asked Freya.

"The clouds?"

Freya nodded.

"I don't know, I like them. When I was ill in bed, I couldn't do much more than stare up at the passing clouds. Sometimes they looked like certain things, you know, a dog, or a duck, or a hand, or something, but sometimes they looked like a whole new world, like a landscape, a huge lake with snow-capped mountains behind, a beach or a valley. I used to imagine castles and kingdoms, and when the sun shone through the grey rain clouds, it just looked like magic…"

Alice waved her hands and the clouds on her horizon turned into a majestic headland, topped with a fairytale castle, and waves beating against the shore down below. She tipped her hand and they were bathed in sunlight, gold rays shining down through turret windows and across the landscape.

Freya could imagine the castle; she could see a princess standing on a balcony, a dragon circling in the sky, and a profusion of her favourite blooms filling the courtyard…

"It is magic isn't it?" said Alice.

Freya nodded, quite enchanted.

"I could stay here forever," said Alice.

"And me," agreed Freya.

Alice smiled with contentment. "*This* is my wonderland."

TWENTY-FOUR
POOLSIDE

Branches hung low and dew dripped from the overhanging leaves as Freya, Jake and Alice ambled through the woods. Mist weaved through the trees, decorating leaves and blossom, and leaving crystals threaded through their tresses.

They wandered on the boundary of Freya's garden and Alice's clouds, and not far ahead a new land became apparent. Freya frowned and her step faltered. She glanced sideways at Jake and spoke softly. "Yours?"

Jake nodded.

"Not what I expected," said Freya, "but then I did wonder why you'd never taken me there."

Jake walked on and the girls followed. The woods opened and the clouds rolled across freshly mown and manicured open grass. Closely cut lavender made a hedge in front of white hydrangea, pink cistus and ruby weigela shrubs, and they lead the way to the oval pool.

Jake moved lightly across the grass, until he came to the tiled edge of the pool. There, he crouched and let his hand skim the water. Alice sat beside him and dropped her legs over the side and kicked the blue water, grinning as she did so.

Freya remained standing, allowing her eyes to take in the scene she was already so familiar with.

The garden was perfect in every way, perfectly cared for, clean and fresh. The pool looked perfect to dive straight into on a hot, summer's day. Freya took a second look, it was too perfect, for on the terrace, up beside the house, was a patio set, round table, four chairs and an umbrella. Sat at the table, shaded by the parasol was Jake's mum. She sat, one leg hooked over the other, in a navy-blue, one-piece swimming costume, sunglasses pushed back on her head and a cocktail, complete with miniature umbrella, in her hand. Standing behind her, with one hand protectively resting on her shoulder, was Jake's father.

Freya couldn't speak.

"I know," said Jake despondently without looking up from the pool.

"I think you're seriously repressed," said Alice shaking her head, but nobody answered her.

Jake moved to sit hugging his knees to him, and Freya lowered herself at his side. She put her arm around his shoulders and stared at the rippling water.

"You need to go down and see," Freya murmured.

Jake shrugged.

"See what?" asked Alice, "It's all here, recreated in perfection!"

"You just do," said Freya, ignoring Alice.

"I know." Jake nodded. "I know."

"She needs you." Freya's words touched him, and his eyes filled with tears.

"It was my fault," he whispered, "my fault."

"It was an accident." Freya shook her head. "Not anyone's fault."

Alice watched the two of them as they spoke softly.

Freya continued. "You need to set her free, you need to set yourself free."

Jake sighed.

"You need to let go," she said.

"We all have to let go," said Alice.

"Jake, you have to let go, get rid of that guilt, yours and hers…"

"I know…"

"She's not the only one who's stuck," Freya told him, squeezing his shoulders. "You're both trapped."

"Who needs guilt?" Alice shook her head. "I could feel guilty, you know, I ruined my family's lives… I got sick and died, and they're left with the fallout. I'm up here sunning myself! I could feel guilty, but *I* didn't cause it, *I* didn't do anything to get sick, it just happened. It's how we all deal with it that matters…"

Freya nodded vigorously. "That's what life is about, how we deal with what's thrown at us."

Alice kicked the water, sending waves across the pool. "If I felt guilty, I would shrivel up, but I'm not, I fought it and tried, and it just didn't work out, but it's no one's fault. Mum once said, when I was crying and scared, she said, 'Just be…' that's all 'Just be,' it's good advice."

"Just be…" repeated Freya thoughtfully. "Just go…"

Jake pushed his hair away from his face and nodded. "I know."

TWENTY-FIVE
FLOUR

As Rachel ran her fingers gently across the books on the shelf, Freya concentrated hard on trying to influence her choice. Rachel thoughtfully pulled one or two partially out, and glanced at them before pushing them back in again.

Jasmine sighed and then grunted. "Book, Mummy," she pleaded, crossing her arms over her chest in a quick, sulky movement, reminiscent of Freya.

Her mum smiled wryly and allowed her finger to hover over a green spine. She lingered before popping out the book. Freya punched the air!

Rachel smiled as she contemplated the woven cover; the sleeve had been worn, torn and lost many years ago. It was an old book, much loved during her own childhood, and in turn adored by Freya. A book she hadn't touched in almost a year, and as there was no picture on the front it held little interest for young Jasmine.

Her daughter watched, her sulky face growing darker. She wanted the baby panda book again…

Rachel flipped open the book and regarded the rudimentary illustrations, and read the opening verse to herself. In her head she saw Freya crouched at her feet, eyes gleaming with anticipation and face ready to mimic the little girl in the book…

She turned the page and read silently; totally oblivious to the glare sent her way from the floor. Rachel thumbed a few pages more then laughed. "Angry! Oh Freya could do that one!" She glanced at Jasmine, "And, I see, so can you!"

She chuckled and turned to show Jasmine a picture of a little girl looking angry. Jasmine already demonstrated a lovely imitation, but her angry look turned to one of interest and Jasmine smiled.

"No, look angry!" prompted Rachel. Jasmine did, and her mum turned the page. "Now look silly." Encouraged by the illustration, Jasmine giggled then did as she was told. "Now happy." Rachel was animated and her memories of Freya now swelled as Jasmine's efforts joined them.

Rachel moved quickly to the sofa and Jasmine followed, both glued to the book. Rachel read and her daughter copied the faces as requested, until Rachel turned a page near to the end, and a scrap of paper slipped out.

She paused and the paper, still folded carefully in half, fell into her lap. She held the book in one hand and touched the corner of the paper with the other. She gently lifted the folded edge and glanced beneath it. Her face paled and she let the edge close.

Jasmine stared expectantly and Rachel met her daughter's eyes. She smiled and turned back to the task in hand, reading again. Her heart wasn't in it, but Jasmine didn't notice as she revelled in the conclusion.

As her mother closed the book, Jasmine reached for it. "Carefully," warned her mother. "Careful with it, it's one of Mum's best books."

Jasmine nodded and took it reverently then moved across the carpet to study the pictures on her own.

Rachel touched the piece of paper in her lap. If the book had brought back memories, the writing on the scrap of paper relinquished an onslaught.

Freya's seven-year-old handwriting, large and round, stared up at her from the torn notepaper. Rachel took a deep breath and steeled herself to read the untidy, childish script that now presented itself. The title announced itself boldly:

'Things to Do.'

1. Go to the park.
2. Make a Sandcastl.
3. Make A choclat cake.
4. Paint.
5. Plant flowers.
6. Give flowers to Daisy.
7. Have Choclate.
8. More Choclate!
9. Paddl in the Sea.
10. Make a Rainbow.

by Freya

Rachel's hand shook.

The doorbell rang, and Rachel almost dropped the paper. She didn't move for a moment then the bell rang again and Jasmine stood up. "Door?" she said and pointed.

Rachel came to her senses and stood, somehow making her way to the front door. Olivia, Steph and Meg stood on the doorstep, and the girls immediately made their way inside much to Jasmine's delight. Olivia noticed the dazed look on Rachel's face and sent the girls upstairs. "Go play for a bit," she told them and ushered Rachel back to her sofa.

They sat and Olivia noted the paper in her friend's hand. "Are you okay?" she asked. Rachel nodded. "What's that then?" asked Olivia, lightly touching the paper.

Rachel handed it over. Olivia gently opened it and let her eyes flicker across the page. "Freya?"

Rachel nodded again and took the page back. "It just brought it all back… I found a book, one of Freya's favourites and I read it to Jasmine, and near the back I found this."

"In the book?"

"Mmm, just sitting there."

"And?" prompted Olivia.

"What d'you mean *and*?" asked Rachel.

"What are you going to do with it?"

"Keep it, what else," Rachel smiled as she studied the childish scrawl.

"And?"

Rachel glanced at Olivia in confusion. "And what? What else d'you want me to do with it?"

Olivia sighed and shook her head as if she was talking to a child herself. "Look, see what it says, *Things to do*… Are you going to do them?"

"Do them?" queried Rachel, the thought to *do* anything hadn't occurred to her.

"These are Freya's *things to do*, her list, it might help to actually do them," said Olivia.

Rachel was quiet for a moment, and she bit her lip as she examined the words. "I haven't been to the park…since…"

Olivia squeezed her hand. "What are you waiting for?"

"I don't know." Rachel's eyes filled with tears, "I just can't go there. Not yet."

"Number two?"

"A sandcastle?" Rachel smiled, "I'll make one next time we go to the beach."

"And number three? Have you got any eggs?"

"Eggs?"

"For a chocolate cake."

Rachel's eyebrows rose. "Now?"

"Yes, now!" said Olivia, "Put the note somewhere safe, and let's get to it. If Freya wants a chocolate cake, then she's going to get a chocolate cake! A huge one with all the extras!"

Moments later Olivia was raiding her friend's kitchen cupboards, and Rachel was watching, her heart beating and her hands shaking.

"Flour?"

Rachel pointed to a shelf in the corner. "Up there, on top."

Olivia paused. "You okay? Do you want me to stop?"

Rachel shook her head, and a small tear slipped out of her eye. She brushed it away quickly. "No, I want to do this, I really do. It's just that it feels like she's here, and…"

"And if I get the flour and sprinkle it all over the room, she'll appear, a little flour-coated ghost!"

"Sort of!" laughed Rachel as Olivia reached up to the shelf.

Soon the kitchen was a whirl of activity as the two women measured butter, flour, sugar, broke chocolate, and cracked eggs. They stirred and beat, and whipped up a frenzy, and the kitchen was filled with giggles and laughter.

Amidst it all, stood Freya, twirling in the centre of the kitchen, trying to catch the mists of flour and reveal herself.

All too soon and the cake was in the oven. The two friends ignored the mess and retired to the lounge, and neither saw the hilarious image that was Freya, attempting to leave floury footprints across the carpet.

Later, when the doorbell rang again, Rachel and Olivia were by the oven. Uncle Pete joined the women and grinned as he took in the chaos that used to be the kitchen.

"We're making a cake for Freya," Rachel told him.

Pete didn't even flinch, just smiled as if it were the most normal activity in the world.

"We need…more chocolate," said Olivia.

"More?" Uncle Pete was surprised. "Looks like you've got the whole sweet shop in here already!"

"We've got enough," said Rachel.

"There is something else…" said Pete. He picked up his helmet and took up a Schwarzenegger pose. "I'll be back," he said with a grin then he disappeared out the back door.

"Your brother *is* something else…" said Olivia with a suggestive raised eyebrow as he powered up his motorbike and sped off down the road.

Rachel grinned, and she continued whipping cream as Olivia smothered the base with strawberry jam. She kept back half of the cream and sifted cocoa into it.

"You got a piping bag?" asked Olivia.

Rachel nodded. "I have, but I've never used it!"

"Let's get it out then, I'll show you." And she did.

When Pete returned, Rachel had a smudge of cream on her nose and Olivia had piped little rosettes all the way up her arm. Pete chuckled when Olivia offered him her arm. "Taste," she ordered. He reddened but obliged, much to Olivia's delight. "Just one." He held up his hand when she offered again. She shrugged and moved back to the cake.

Pete took off his gloves and pulled a little packet out of his jacket. "Chocolate Stars, for our little star. She loved them. And I hope she's watching up there, somewhere in the Milky Way!"

Rachel's eyes misted over again. "They were her favourites."

She opened the packet and placed them carefully around Olivia's piped swirls. Then she stood back, and Pete put his arm around her. "Are you going to tell me why?" asked her brother.

"Why what?" came a gruff voice as Joe wandered through the back door into the floury kitchen. "Chocolate cake!" He gave his wife a kiss and stretched out his hand towards the cake, only to receive a sharp slap on the back of his hand from Olivia. He grinned then offered a hurt expression. "It's not for me then?"

Rachel disappeared and retrieved Freya's list from behind her photograph. She placed it softly in her husband's hand. "It's for Freya, it's number three."

His eyes glistened as he read the note in his daughter's familiar prose. He nodded and glanced up at Rachel. He gently wiped the smudge of cream from his wife's nose and kissed it lightly. "It's perfect, heavenly even…"

Freya sashayed across the dusty white kitchen floor and leaned against the counter. As her father kissed her mother once more, she grinned and dipped her finger into a creamy swirl. She left no impression, but she put her finger into her mouth and her memory let her taste buds explode with chocolaty glory.

She lingered by the cake as her family and friends moved out of the room, and traced imaginary shapes in the flour-dusted worktop.

Much, much later, after the cake had been devoured and Rachel was cleaning up, she paused for just a moment, before wiping the washcloth over the surface, and considered the child-like heart left in the residual flour…

TWENTY-SIX
COINCIDENCE

Freya knew that Uncle Pete wished he had a heated seat and handlebars on his bike because he had just told his sister so. He'd pulled his neck tube up over his chin and mouth and put on his helmet, and Freya had followed. The chilly March draughts did not put her off riding pillion.

And without even a sneaking suspicion of a passenger, Uncle Pete did not hold back once he was on the road.

Freya allowed her hair to flow behind her and she moved with the motorbike, feeling the thrill in her head as she leaned side to side with the machine. She let Uncle Pete's oblivion drive her, and today she was looking forward to a long ride.

She was, therefore, disappointed when after a few streets the revs lowered and Pete pulled to a halt just past a woman walking down the street. He glanced back over his shoulder and Freya noted his pupils dilate in his friendly green eyes. He unbuckled his helmet, slipped it off and rested it between his legs on the front of the bike. He revved the bike then turned it off. He glanced casually back again and Freya grinned as her unflappable Uncle Pete actually blushed and licked his lips nervously.

She twisted on the bike to face backwards and watched as the object of his affection walked towards them.

Jen's red hair glimmered in the bright sun and her hand moved self-consciously towards her face. She swept her hair back and then looked down at her feet, but even Freya could see the lift in her step. Jen's hair fell across her cheek and again she moved it as she reached the bike.

"Hey," greeted Pete.

Jen smiled. "Hi." The wind blew wildly and Jen pulled her coat tighter around her. "Cold isn't it?" she offered.

Pete nodded and ran his fingers through his shaggy hair. "Where are you off to today then?" he asked.

"Oh, just off to see a friend."

His eyebrows rose in interest. "Anyone I know?"

She shrugged. "I don't think so…Oh, yes, you do…remember old Thomas?"

He frowned, not recognising the name.

"Yes, you do…at the shop, the old man who loved your bike, way back, last autumn."

Pete thought hard, willing himself to remember.

Jen continued. "When I first met you, you were buying milk…"

Pete smiled, happy that she could recall the first time they had met, then he trawled back into his memory banks. "Yes! I remember, old Mr Thomas…"

"Thomas Hillman, Mr Hillman."

"Yes, Thomas, he had an old Bonneville, an old Triumph!" Pete recollected.

"That's right, and he wanted a go on yours, on this!" said Jen, tapping the back of Pete's bike.

"He did? He did, yes, he did mention it. He's getting on a bit though isn't he?"

"I didn't say you *should* let him have a go!" Jen laughed.

"So why are you going to see him?"

"I'm not, I like to spend time with his wife, she's teaching me how to sew."

Pete laughed, and Jen took a mock hurt stance. "Thanks very much!" she said, "I'll have you know I can sew on a button now!"

"Very good, you'll make someone a good wife one day," quipped Pete.

Jen smiled, reddened and stared at her shoes. Pete sobered and stuttered. "I, I mean, you know…"

Jen glanced up at him and met his eyes. "Yes, I will one day, when the right man comes along and sweeps me off my feet." She laughed.

There was an awkward silence for a moment, when Jen's watch became very interesting, and Pete's bike needed a quick polish then Jen spoke. "You could come with me you know, Thomas would love to see the bike again…"

Pete looked up at her.

"I mean, if you're not on your way somewhere…" She shook her head noncommittally.

"No, I'm not going anywhere, I could come," he said.

There was another moment of silence.

"I've not got another helmet at the moment…" he began.

"That's okay, I'm not going on the bike!" She smiled.

"Where do they live then?"

Jen grinned. "I'll meet you there," she told him. "Start up the bike…"

Pete did and glanced at her expectantly.

"And your helmet, got to be safe you know."

He put the helmet back on and revved the engine. He stared at her through the raised visor.

"It's a pretty house, not far…" she began walking.

Pete kicked up the stand and moved the bike forward.

She walked briskly.

"How far?" asked Pete, keeping up.

"Not far, be careful driving."

"It's riding," he corrected her, "not driving…"

"Okay, be careful, on that big bike…"

"Are you going to tell me where we're going then?" he asked, braking as he moved ahead of her.

Jen kept walking, catching up and moving on. "C'mon," she said.

Pete grinned inside his helmet and revved hard. He glanced over his shoulder and moved out, away from the kerb. He rode down the road a little further then pulled in again to wait. When she didn't catch up he looked behind and saw her standing by a gate. She waved and opened the gate with a big smile.

Pete felt his heart flutter as he watched her and Freya knew he was wondering whether to follow or not. Freya slipped off the bike. Pete chuckled and waved back then shot away and off down the road. Freya laughed as Pete disappeared. The motorbike roared and faded just as the smile did on Jen's face.

Jen faltered, her hand on the gate and her eyes staring down the road. Freya stood beside her and could hear Jen's heart as it beat faster than usual.

"Hello dear," came Mrs Hillman's voice from the door. "Hello Jen."

Jen wiped the crestfallen look from her face and replaced it with a big smile. "Hi Joan." Jen glanced back down the road one more time, before closing the gate and moving up the path.

Freya stood at the gatepost, and from there she watched as Jen's ears picked up the buzz of a motorbike as it returned up the street. She saw Jen's shoulders rise and heard the little sigh that escaped her lips. Jen held herself and smiled at Joan, but didn't turn as the bike purred on the kerb.

"Hi Jen!" came Pete's muffled voice, "Fancy seeing you here!"

Jen's smile grew and her heart felt like it would burst, and even Mrs Hillman could see the flush that spread across Jen's cheeks.

Jen composed herself and turned, catching Pete's eye as he lifted his visor. "Hey Pete, what a coincidence!"

Joan Hillman sensed the start of something special, and was unable to resist. "Hello, young man, do you know Jen? Would you like to come and join us? I've been baking this morning."

Freya looked beyond Mrs Hillman and saw old Thomas, alerted by the sound of a meaty motorbike, hurrying down the side passage of the house.

"It's the bike!" he grinned in delight. "Save us some cakes, biscuits, whatever you've been baking, but we'll be out here a while!"

Joan huffed and waved her hand, dismissing her husband as he reached the motorbike. "We won't see them for hours dear," she said and she ushered Jen indoors.

Joan did not see the glance that Jen cast behind her, but Freya did, and Freya felt her heart leap in exactly the same way Jen's did.

TWENTY-SEVEN
DEEPER

The sweet smell of cupcakes pervaded the house, a sugary, fresh baked fragrance, tinged with citrus. Joan guided Jen into the kitchen. "The icing," she told her, "takes the edge off the sweetness, one last thing…" Joan picked up a half-skinned lemon and continued grating it. "Looks good too," she said as she sprinkled sunshine-yellow rind over the top of the lemon icing.

"You should teach me to cook as well as to sew," Jen said as she accepted a cake. "Oooh, heavenly…" she murmured.

"Is there a reason you should be able to cook then?" probed Joan.

"Oh…" Jen shook her head, wiping lemon off her lip. "I *can* cook, just can't bake. I'm useless with cakes."

"Anytime you need a cake…*any* cake, *big* or small…" hinted Joan, "Just come to me."

Freya stood at the kitchen door, reminiscing. She remembered standing in that doorway a couple of years ago, having followed her nose down several streets. She recalled Mrs Hillman's cakes and pastries and puddings from a variety of church functions. Her favourite had been an evening of puddings, most donated by Mrs Hillman, and Freya had moved from one to the next, trying a spoonful of each, and so on all evening. Chocolate fudge cake, raspberry cheesecake, lemon meringue, a divine strawberry Pavlova, cookies, honeycomb ice-cream…the list went on, and Freya could almost taste the light, crumbly, lemony sponge as it disappeared into Jen's mouth.

Freya blinked and moved to Uncle Pete's motorbike.

"It purred like the proverbial cat…" Mr Hillman mused, "No, more like a tiger, it had bite…"

"This roars…like a lion," said Pete.

"Like a dragon!" Thomas laughed and patted the machine's engine.

"Did you have it long?"

"Oh years and years, they were built to last in those days." Thomas stared at the bike. "Lots of elbow grease and hard work, I spent many a day brandishing a chamois!"

"When were you last on a bike?" asked Pete. Thomas's eyes brightened and his smile broadened, and Pete felt slightly guilty at having asked the question.

"Not for many years now, but," He glanced at Pete. "I never give up hope."

Pete changed the subject. "What are you driving now?"

Thomas smiled wistfully and kept his eyes trained on Pete for a moment longer than was comfortable. Then he indicated the kerbside behind the bike. "This old Toyota, I know it's ancient, but I just don't like the new cars out these days, just don't trust them. It's like me, it's old, it's going nowhere fast, but it's reliable. I trust it."

Pete grinned.

"It's got a tape player, and a radio, none of that new-fangled stuff, mp-thingamabobs, and," he added insistently, "I don't need satellites to show me where to go either!"

"Have you got far to go then?"

Thomas looked pensive. "I must be a Thursday's child…"

Pete frowned, not comprehending Thomas's reticence. A brisk wind kicked up and Thomas shivered. "Let's go inside," said Pete, placing his hand on Thomas's arm. Up to a moment ago the old man had looked strong and robust, but within a single instant he had changed and now appeared both frail and fragile. Pete helped the old man down the path.

They walked down the side passage and to the back door. Pete glanced at the immaculate garden, full of yellow daffodils and vibrant tulips, all swaying in the wind, and he could not associate the garden with this feeble man gripping his arm.

The back door opened and Jen invited them in. As Thomas stepped over the threshold his whole persona changed much to Pete's astonishment. Pete caught Jen's eye and he understood her concern. Freya watched as the couple connected on a deeper level and they both eyed Thomas with a new outlook.

Thomas moved across the kitchen floor with a spring in his step and he cheekily smacked his wife's bottom, moving his other hand over her shoulder to steal a cupcake. She beat him to it and rapped his knuckles. He cried out and jumped back, and Joan turned to grin at him. He leaned forward and kissed her.

"Now leave them alone until I tell you otherwise." She scolded. "What am I going to do with you?"

She turned back to her cakes.

Thomas chuckled and turned back to Pete and Jen. He made light of his wife's reprimand, but both Pete and Jen could see a physical pain that coursed through his body. They could see it every time he moved, every time he carefully positioned himself, and every time he checked himself.

Freya could see deeper still. She could see every physical twinge, but she could also see every emotional twinge, every wrench in his heart and she could hear what no one else could, she could hear his heart breaking…

TWENTY-EIGHT
THE PARK

Rachel stared at Freya's list, unaware that her daughter studied it with her. It was number one that still troubled her, but when the bluebells began to open and nod at her, when fields became blue and woodlands were carpeted, she knew the time had come.

Jasmine clutched a bunch of bluebells tightly in one fist and held Daddy's hand with the other. Rachel walked slightly ahead.

The sun had risen on the horizon and Jasmine yawned, it was still too early for her chatter. She just grasped her flowers and her daddy, and tried to keep up. As Rachel moved ahead, Joe picked up his daughter and carried her. He stopped as they reached the park gates.

He hadn't witnessed the tragedy and the park held no demons for him, but he watched his wife's posture stiffen as she walked right up to the gates.

There were no flowers, no cuddly toys, nothing adorning the gate in Freya's memory.

Rachel reached into her pocket and pulled out a ribbon, a lilac ribbon. Her eyes blurred as she threaded it through the metal bars and her fingers shook, almost uncontrollably, as she tried to tie it.

Joe placed Jasmine on the grass inside the gate and moved to his wife's side. He gently touched Rachel's fingers and cupped her hands in his then he reached out and tied the ribbon. Freya's mother ran her fingers across the bow, letting the satin ribbon slip through her hand, and leaned heavily against her husband. Jasmine moved forward and held out her bluebells. Her mother took her hand and nodded, taking the flowers. She dropped them at the foot of the gate, beneath the ribbon, and stepped back.

Bluebells lay across the pavement, and the ribbon rippled in the breeze just as it had in Freya's ponytail.

TWENTY-NINE
BETWEEN

"You have to come with me." Jake's expression was serious. "I can't do this on my own."

Freya sighed, after seeing her mother's distress, she knew another time had come, and this one was Jake's. "Just close your eyes," she said. His blue eyes pierced her then his eyelids fluttered closed. She took his hand. "Think us there."

The sun beat down upon them, and as they opened their eyes they were flooded with hot summer memories, evoking the smell of the sea, sunscreen, and strangely enough, coconuts.

"Sorry," said Jake, "Mum always used coconut oil sun lotion."

"Don't be sorry," chided Freya, "We're here, where you're meant to be, and your memories match!"

They did, and soon chlorine overtook memories of the beach. The pool glistened and the sunshine shimmered on its gently rippling surface.

Freya glanced at Jake. He was pale and wrung his hands nervously. His eyes, the same colour as the swimming pool, flit back and forth, searching, but not finding.

"She's not here," he said with a trace of relief.

"She's always here," Freya replied.

He scanned the terrace, searched the garden beyond and checked all the plastic sun loungers.

"She's not here," he insisted, "Unless she's hiding on top of a parasol."

Freya threw him an annoyed glare and told him to wait and be patient. "She's here…somewhere."

Jake wasn't so sure. "Would she be in the house?"

Freya shrugged.

Jake took a step forward intending to move to his old house, but a ripple in the pool distracted him. He wandered closer, to the edge, standing on the very tiles that had once ended his life.

He stared beyond the sun's glare and beneath the ripples, to the shape moving across the bottom of the pool.

His mouth dropped and rain began to fall, but as Jake's vision blurred, he realised there was no rain, only his tears, as he stared down into the water at his mother swimming like a mermaid on the bottom.

She weaved and meandered like a fish, her long, white dress clinging to her body, her arms pushing through the water, her head moving side to side like a snake, and her long, fair hair fanning out as she searched every inch of the pool floor.

Then she looked up.

Her desolate face saw Jake through the surface ripples. Her hair undulated as she paused, stunned, staring up in disbelief.

The boy, her son, was falling, replaying the nightmare that haunted her. Her mouth opened but no sound accompanied it, and no bubbles rose. She stared in anguish as Jake slipped into the water.

She kicked her legs and pushed forward as Jake began to sink in a jumble of legs and flailing arms. She hurried through the water, this time she would save him…

His blue eyes found hers and she refused to let go. She surged forward and scooped up the small boy in her outstretched arms.

They were together, finally together, mother and son.

Freya stood, poolside, staring down watching the joyous watery reunion. Jake clung to his mother, and the two bodies rolled and wheeled before rising and punching through the surface.

Freya could barely contain her excitement and helped the two out of the pool. Water slipped off them, and they moved away from the edge, leaving a puddle but no footprints.

Jake's mother stepped back to look at her son then she hugged him to her, unable to let go after so long searching. "Oh Jake, my Jake, my boy…"

They stood like that lost within each other for a long time, his name echoing softly on the breeze.

A sharp click broke the reverie, as the back door to the house opened.

Freya started and took a step away from Jake and his mother. She opened her mouth to speak, but Jake's mum put her finger to her lips, and instead they watched the door.

Dressed in a loose shirt and unflattering cargo shorts, Jake's father stepped out onto his terrace. His head was bowed as he lifted his lighter to the cigarette in his mouth.

Jake ran forward as light as the wind itself, and stood beside his father. The flint sparked and a flame caught. Jake pursed his lips and blew. A brief, but fierce gust brushed the flame and it sputtered out. His Dad flicked the lighter again and lifted it. The draught blew it out again. For the third time, he attempted to light up, but the flame flickered out.

He shook his head and muttered to himself then he glanced up. The pool shimmered in the bright sun and diamonds danced across the calm water.

Suddenly his breath caught, and he coughed, and the cigarette fell from his open mouth. He walked forward, shielding his eyes and staring at the side of his swimming pool. Tears glistened in his eyes, and Freya looked to where he was staring.

Jake and his mother stood, bathed in white sunlight, by the side of the pool.

Freya looked to the approaching man, panic rising, and back again to the two standing still.

Jake's father lifted his hand to his chest, placing it gently over his heart. His heartbeats were audible. His mouth formed a word, but none escaped. He tried again. "Kerry, Jake…" Two words were all that was needed.

Freya's worry turned to wonder, and from wonder to delight.

"Henry," murmured Jake's mother, and Jake whispered. "Dad."

Freya could not contain herself. "He can see you!"

Two pairs of eyes locked with Jake's father and Henry hesitated, just metres from his departed family.

"We're in between," whispered Kerry, "but we're okay, we're alright."

"I can…see you…Kerry," Tears rolled over stubbly cheeks. "Jake! You've grown, oh, how you've grown, my boy…my man."

Freya glanced at Jake and a knife cut through her. Gone was the boy, gone was the seven-year-old, before her stood a young man, grown and gorgeous. If Freya's heart could still beat, it would have stopped, and Freya knew time was short.

"We're alright, we're alright…" echoed Jake's mother.

Freya watched as the sun shone brighter and brighter, until suddenly Jake's father was standing alone, staring at a space beside the swimming pool. He dropped to his knees and wept, and Freya was gone in a flash.

THIRTY
IMPRESSIONS

Such was Freya's anxiety that she couldn't think.

She raced across her garden and dashed though the bluebell swathed woods. Alice's cloudy turrets rose high above the canopy and Freya burst through the last few trees with sobs that nearly choked her. She stopped and bent forward, her breath tearing at her chest. She wiped away tears and shook her head.

She took a deep breath and laughed, and laughed again, hyperventilation taking her to the dizzy heights of hysteria.

She shook her head again and covered her eyes with her hands. "Stop it," she commanded, her trembling voice echoing across the misty landscape. "Just stop it!"

Her head began to clear and her throat stopped burning, memories of running and breathlessness faded and Freya stood alone, surrounded by the edge of her forest and Alice's clouds.

Her tears remained, resting on her face like dewdrops. She wiped them away, but more prickled behind her eyelids, and she wondered at the physical response, she hadn't cried real tears for so long. Now is not the time to question, thought Freya and emptied her mind of everything but Jake.

More tears escaped as she recalled her last image of Jake, standing, full-grown, beside his mother. It shocked her, Jake was her constant, her companion, her everything. Now, because she had encouraged him to face his past, his future had been thrown wide open…

Freya closed her eyes and allowed her soul to guide her.

Jake stood waiting.

He looked no more than seven-years-old and Freya's grin spread across her face. She ran and threw herself at him. "I thought you'd gone! I thought I'd missed you!" she wailed.

"How could I go without waiting for you?" he admonished.

She shook her head and buried it against his shoulder. His shoulders broadened and his arms strengthened and Freya felt eternally safe.

"I would never have gone without you." His voice deepened and Freya moved back in surprise, looking up into his face. His blue eyes stared right back, but they were again set into the face of a young man. "It's difficult to control," he apologised.

She nodded, swallowing the lump in her throat, understanding without the need of explanation. "You're ready."

"I'm more than ready!" He laughed and the timbre of his voice warmed her soul.

"You waited…for me," she spoke softly.

"Always," he replied.

Freya reached up on tiptoes and kissed his cheek. "Look! I'm crying!" she said with incredulity.

He smiled. "I'll leave you with one last thing…" he began, "learn a little more, and you'll have more control, there is so much more to learn, you're not even using half your brain at the moment! At those, these, peaks of emotion, you can leave impressions…like tears, ripples on the water…it's not just memories you can evoke!" Jake bent and kissed the top of Freya's head, "You can do anything, be anything…"

Freya nodded and hugged him once more then she stepped back and for the first time took in her surroundings.

The immaculate lawn was still bordered by shrubs and the lavender path still snaked across the grass, but Jake's house had vanished. The swimming pool began the same as it always had, but the white tiles turned into quartz and then into granite rocks, and the calm pool rolled over the edge of a precipice into a roiling waterfall.

Jake waved and dived into the swimming pool, darting through the water like a dolphin. He flipped right over the edge and let the waterfall take him.

Freya, accompanied by Alice, Keira and all their friends, hurried to the edge and watched as the foaming flume took him into the stream below.

The stream widened and Jake floated down the serpentine river. The river flowed flanked by beautiful granite rocks at the water's edge, and then between fresh green meadows. Jake swam, flitting to and fro in the frothing water.

Far, far ahead, beyond a curve in the winding waterway and woodland swathed in blue, stood a willow, pale green against the bright, white light. Jake powered through the water and a figure beneath the tree leapt into the river. Jake swam to meet his mother and they both climbed ashore.

They walked on, through daisy-filled meadows, to the willow. The meadow filled with a pure, encompassing, white light, and when the willow reappeared standing alone, Freya smiled. She knew that a serpentine river now flowed alongside her willow and white roses, and that wherever he was, Jake would wait.

THIRTY-ONE
PAINTING

Laughter filled the house, along with a golden ray of sunshine peering in through the dining room window. The late afternoon sun rested on Jasmine's animated face, and her mother leaned across the table to lift Jasmine's fair hair out of her way. Jasmine beamed at her mother and turned back to her fingers. She plunged her index finger into a pot of green paint and giggled.

"Squishy!" Her father grinned at her and across the table he stuck his finger into crimson paint. Together they lifted their fingers and brandished them in the air.

"Careful," said Rachel.

Oblivious her husband and daughter stabbed at the clean white paper before them. Jasmine's giggles filled the air and Rachel pulled up a chair to sit with her family at the table.

Jasmine threw caution to the wind and plunged her whole fist into the blue pot. "That's the spirit Jaz!" cried Joe, "Go for it!"

Rachel watched and bit her lip, trying to ignore the accumulating mess. Joe glanced at her, and allowed himself a smile. "Rachel, grab a piece of paper, c'mon liberate yourself!"

His wife glared at him.

Jasmine's paper was a blobby, crumpled mess of blue and green.

"What are you drawing then?" asked Dad.

"Blue Ted," she replied with a satisfied nod. "Blue Ted."

"I'm painting you!" Her father told her.

"Me!" squealed Jasmine climbing up onto her knees and leaning across the table. Joe picked up the page and showed his daughter the rudimentary red face and big smile, two spots of green for her eyes and yellow for her hair. "It's me!" she screeched, "Jasmine!"

Mum pulled Jasmine's picture out from beneath her and laid it on the floor by the back door. She gave her daughter another piece of paper. Jasmine made herself busy with a mixture of red and blue handprints.

Rachel watched her husband as he dipped his finger back into the red paint and drew another circle on the page beside Jasmine. Two more green dots for eyes and then he opened a pot of brown. Rachel stiffened and got up, she moved across the room and into the kitchen. Sitting on top of the breadbin was Freya's list complete with a smudge of chocolate. "Number four, Freya," she whispered, "painting…" Rachel moved to the windowsill still holding the list. She picked up a paper cup, decorated with yellow poster paint spots and green squiggles. "Number five, Jasmine's sunflower."

Her mind backtracked and she recalled the leader of Jasmine's playgroup pulling out a packet of sunflower seeds. The toddlers painted the paper cups then their mums filled each pot with compost, and each child pushed a sunflower seed, or two, into the cup. Then the children were read a book about a giant sunflower, that grew and grew and grew, and no one could see the top. Then Jasmine had commented that her big sister, Freya, loved sunflowers and she was probably going to be found at the top!

Rachel wandered back to the dining table and smiled as Joe held up his painting. Jasmine squealed again. "Me and Feya! Me and Feya!"

Joe nodded. "You and Freya. Aren't you beautiful?"

Jasmine nodded then moved back to her painting. She stuck out her tongue as she concentrated and dragged her fingers across the page. Her mother smiled at the huge churned up swirl of muddy colours, and finally relaxed.

She pulled out her own piece of paper and sat down. She picked up the pot of brown and dipped in her finger. She pressed the tip onto the middle of the page and made a dot, she carried on and made a big circle of little brown spots. She washed her finger in the tub of water and reached for the yellow. She plunged her finger in with more gusto this time and smiled.

"Feels good, doesn't it?" Her husband grinned at her.

She nodded and put finger to paper. Petals appeared surrounding the brown centre, long, thin, bright yellow petals. She mixed a little brown into her yellow and dabbed thin lines on some of the petals, to add depth, and then went for the green. She painted a long stem and big green leaves.

Jasmine bent forwards, tipping her chair, as she looked at her mother's picture. "Feya's sunfower," she said.

Behind her mother, Freya shook her head, and Rachel echoed her oldest daughter's thoughts.

"No, sweetheart, Jasmine's sunflower."

THIRTY-TWO
DISTANT STAR

"Number four..." said Rachel holding up the painting of her two daughters.

"Wow! Jasmine's quite the artist, brilliant for a two-year-old!" exclaimed Olivia.

"Joe painted that!" Rachel laughed.

"And you, what did you paint?"

Rachel pointed to the sunflower fixed to the freezer.

"I like that, you *are* good," praised her friend.

Rachel shrugged. "Jasmine did loads, got really carried away!" She pointed to a mass of crinkled sheets of paper covered with messy swirls, smears and blobs, held precariously by an assortment of fridge magnets.

Olivia hugged Rachel. "You did it together, and that's what counts. And the rest of the list?"

Freya's mother glanced up at the list, now mounted on a piece of purple card and pinned to the notice board. Freya smiled; only the most important notices got pride of place on Mum's home-made corkboard.

"I did go back to the park...just the once, on the anniversary,"

"It'll get easier," offered Olivia.

"We made a cake," Rachel placed an invisible tick beside Freya's number three with her finger. "And at Christmas we bought all Freya's favourite chocolates, and stuffed our faces, that, and the cake, more than covers seven and eight!" She moved her finger down the list. "Painting, flowers, we've never stopped giving Daisy flowers, she always takes them even when the stems are too short and the flowers are squashed!"

"So you're left with two, nine and ten." Olivia read.

"Jasmine painted a rainbow, does that count?"

Olivia frowned. "Not sure."

"We've never made a sandcastle, you know, a real one, we've dumped buckets of sand upside down, but,"

"I think she meant something more adventurous," interrupted Olivia, "turrets, moats and a drawbridge, that sort of thing."

"Mmm."

"Decorated with shells and flags and lolly sticks. Is Pete going to help?"

"Maybe."

"I like building castles, never made a big sandcastle, but I did make a huge cardboard one for school, when I was about twelve."

Rachel glanced at Olivia. "You need to give up on Pete."

"Never give up," said Olivia pursing her lips.

"You'll have to this time."

"Go on."

"He's besotted with Jen, you know, the red-head from the Post Office."

"He is?" Olivia pouted then shrugged. "All's fair in love and war."

"Sorry Liv, you don't stand a chance, she's really lovely, really nice…Liv! I didn't mean it that way, you're lovely too, I just meant…"

"It's okay," Olivia grinned, "I'm only teasing! It was a long shot, he's just so cute!"

"He's my brother!"

"Doesn't stop him being cute!"

"You'd scare the life out of him!" Rachel giggled.

"Me? Scare a big, butch biker?"

Rachel nodded. "He's really into the damsel in distress thing, you really aren't! Not that there are any damsels in distress these days, but he sees that big bike of his as a knight's charger..."

"The knight in shining armour routine..." Olivia sighed wistfully. "We could all do with one of those." She stared out at the garden. "So changing the subject...how's Jasmine's sunflower doing? I've never managed to keep anything from school alive. Once it's left the confines of the classroom, and the safety of the school gate, it wilts and dies...sunflowers, runner-bean seedlings, can't even grow mustard and cress! I even managed to drop the jelly Steph brought out in a yoghurt pot!"

Rachel never got to reply as Olivia moved from the dining room into the lounge. Rachel followed and grinned. Despite the change of subject Olivia lifted the lace curtain and peered out of the window.

"It's the knight's steed, carrying not only the knight, but the princess too. Any chance I can cut off Rapunzel's glorious locks?" Olivia let the curtain drop and turned to Rachel, she grimaced then laughed. "It's okay, really! I'm not jealous, well only a little bit...I wish them both the best of luck!"

Rachel lightly punched her friend's arm. "She *is* really nice..."

"So am I," replied Olivia. "Maybe you've got another brother..."

Rachel laughed as she went to open the door. "Not that I know of!" She threw the door open with a smile. "Hi Pete, Jen."

Pete was half way up the steps with his motorbike helmet tucked under his arm. He glanced back and waited for Jen. Jen struggled with the chinstrap on her helmet and he moved back to her and unfastened it. Jen lifted the helmet off and self-consciously touched her hair. Pete leaned to her and whispered in her ear, Jen blushed and Rachel grinned.

They made it up the steps and in through the front door. Jen wasn't sure where to put her helmet, but Pete took it for her. Rachel ushered them inside and raised her eyes over Pete's shoulder at Olivia. Olivia smiled brightly, and Pete grasped Jen's hand.

"I wouldn't have taken you for a biker," Olivia smiled as Jen shook out her auburn hair.

Jen grinned back. "Nor would I until a week or two ago, now I can see the attraction!"

"Getting one of your own then?" asked Olivia.

Pete nodded vigorously. "Oh, I bet she will!"

Jen reddened. "I think I'm quite happy riding behind you at the moment, it's far too big for me!"

"You look good in the gear," Rachel told her.

"Very good..." Pete nudged her.

"Thank you," said Jen graciously.

"Maybe I should get some leathers..." Olivia gave a wicked grin. "The last time I rode was years and years ago."

"I never had, 'til Pete took me out, I always said I wouldn't! Don't think Mum likes me on it!" Jen admitted.

"Oh, it's great fun!" vouched Olivia.

"It *is*!" agreed Jen. "I had no idea! Now I know why old Thomas wants another go!"

"Old Thomas?" said Rachel, "You don't mean Thomas Hillman do you?"

Pete nodded. "He's asked, and he's not shy about it either!"

"But he's ancient!" exclaimed Olivia.

"You can't let him!" objected Rachel, "Far too dangerous."

"I didn't say I was letting him," said Pete.

Olivia cocked her head to one side. "Why not?"

"You're asking 'why not'?" exclaimed Rachel. "You just said he was ancient!"

"Why not? Yes, he's old, but why shouldn't he get another chance?" Olivia shook her head, "Who are we to deny an old man his dream?"

Jen looked thoughtful. "I used to think it would be too dangerous, but…"

Rachel shook her head briskly. "Don't even go there, Jen let me take your gloves and jacket."

Jen glanced at Pete as she took off one glove and gave it to Rachel. As she slid off the second glove Rachel drew in her breath.

"Oh Jen, Oh Pete!" Rachel dropped the glove and grabbed Jen's left hand. "Oh wow!"

"Let me see," said Olivia with a wry smile. "Oh that's gorgeous, beautiful!"

Pete cleared his throat. "That's what we were stopping by for."

Rachel still clutched Jen's hand and excitement filled her voice. "Bridesmaids, flowers, cake…"

"To the first question…Jasmine," began Pete, "If that's okay?"

Rachel's eyes filled with tears. "Jasmine will love it! I'm just… it's just…"

Pete took his sister's hand. "I know, I know Freya always wanted to be a bridesmaid…"

"Yours, she always wanted to be yours…" said Rachel.

"I know," Pete picked up his jacket and reached into his pocket. "That's why we got this."

"At the same time as we got the ring." Jen smiled.

Pete pulled out a little jewellery box and opened it. Rachel took it. "Open the locket," her brother told her.

Rachel took the silver locket in her fingers, undid the catch and gasped. Inside, a tiny picture of Freya grinned up at her. The same photograph that sat atop the mantelpiece, hint of fairy wings and all.

"It's an early gift for Jasmine so both sisters will be with us on the day." Jen touched Rachel's shoulder.

Freya ducked under her mother's arms and stared at the locket. Her picture stared back and Freya laughed. Goosebumps appeared on Rachel's arms and she hugged her brother and kissed Jen. "Thank you, thank you…"

"Look on the front," said Pete. "It's a star, for our distant star, Freya."

Not so distant, thought Freya and she leaned forward to kiss the cold metal. Freya's kiss was calculated to leave an impression, and for one moment every heart in the room skipped a beat, caught up in Freya's tingling aura.

THIRTY-THREE
WILLOW

Jake's river cut across the countryside, gushing through a rocky outcrop and curving with the riverbank, until it flowed steadily and peacefully at the foot of Freya's willow. It gurgled over pebbles and splashed against the grassy verge, and pooled beside the embankment.

The tree bent and dipped its fronds allowing the water to ripple and tease its narrow leaves, and Freya dabbled her toes. Rounded Hebe bushes and white roses bloomed, lending a beautiful fragrance to the air whenever Freya retreated there.

The scent of roses filled Freya's mind as she sat, with the river tickling her feet, beneath the willow.

She felt incredibly lonely.

Memories of Jake coursed through her mind getting mixed up with thoughts of her mother, excitement from Uncle Pete's news and concerns about old Thomas. She was relieved when Alice stepped through the tree's hanging boughs and sat down beside her.

They sat in silence listening only to the murmur of the stream. They did not need to speak; Alice understood only too well, every notion that swirled in Freya's mind.

Voices could be heard a little while later and soon the shade beneath the tree was filled with friendly faces.

"We wondered where you were hiding," said Keira.

"I'm not hiding," she replied.

"You're missing Jake," Ben spoke softly and Freya smiled at him.

She nodded and brought her feet up out of the water. She bent her knees and held them to her chest, resting her chin on them. "I am."

"You know he's waiting, don't you?" said Sophie.

Freya nodded again.

"You know you're almost ready, don't you?" Sophie continued.

Freya's eyes widened. "You can tell?"

Sophie nodded.

"How?" demanded Freya, "I don't feel like I'm ready."

"I can just tell," Sophie shrugged. "I'm ready, maybe that's why I can tell."

"Are you going?" asked Freya.

"She's waiting for Ben," Keira said.

"How can you wait and still be here?" asked Freya, confusion clouding her mind. "Jake didn't wait here, for me."

"He couldn't, his mother needed him," replied Sophie. "I can wait as there's no one waiting for me on the other side."

"We're going to go together." Ben smiled and grasped Sophie's hand tightly. Sophie returned his smile and gave him a motherly hug.

"But you *are* almost ready," she told Freya.

Freya's gaze moved back to the water. "My mother still hurts…"

"You'll find the answer," Keira told her, "We all will."

Freya watched the ripples.

"I'll tell you something else…" began Sophie.

"I already know…" Freya paused for a moment. "Thomas is almost ready too."

THIRTY-FOUR
CHICKEN SOUP

It disturbed Freya, the fact that she appeared to know that old Thomas had little time left, but she wasn't the only one who knew…

Freya sought refuge with Pete and Jen, and accompanied them to the Hillman's home. Jen was surprised when Joan opened the door with a twinkle in her eye.

"You can go on up and see Thomas, he's a bit poorly today, but I've got visitors…I'll be up when his chicken soup's ready." Joan grinned.

Jen followed the delicious smell of the broth and stuck her head round the kitchen door. She smiled as Mrs Feldman and Mrs Taylor waved and greeted her. "Hello ladies," she said as Joan shuffled back to the table laden with cups and cakes.

"Carol and Linda thought it was about time they popped by to sample my cakes," Joan teased.

"Oh now, Joan, you know that's not true!" Mrs Taylor laughed loudly.

"But they are amazing!" put in Mrs Feldman, "Well worth the visit!"

The three ladies laughed and Jen bid a hasty retreat.

Pete made a face and Jen grinned as they made their way up the stairs. Mr Hillman's deep voice floated down the stairwell. "He's singing, he can't be that bad!" Jen whispered. She knocked and gently pushed open the bedroom door.

The curtains were half-closed and Thomas lay on the bed covered by a floral eiderdown and propped up by a multitude of pastel-coloured, frilled pillows. He looked pale, but beamed at them as they entered, his smile lighting the room far more than the dim afternoon light trying to get through the heavy curtains did.

"Thomas, are you okay?" Jen asked.

"Just a bit rough today, we all have our off days. I'm glad you came."

"Can't let you down Tom," said Pete, "What's up then?"

Jen shot Pete a furious glare.

"Just the usual, a bit achy, maybe flu or something."

"Is your back playing up again?" Pete asked ignoring Jen.

Thomas nodded.

"Can you get up?"

"Too painful today." He grimaced as he tried to lift himself higher, but the pain was too great and his arms shook with the effort.

"Let me help," insisted Pete moving to Thomas's side and carefully lifting him, and placing him against the pillows.

"Thank you," said Thomas. He stretched out his hand, but Jen was there quicker. "Let me," she said as she picked up a box of tablets from his bedside. "How many?"

"Just one," said Thomas.

"Co-codamol," said Jen glancing at him. "These are strong."

"Good," replied Thomas.

She reached for a second box at the rear of the table, half hidden by an open book. She read the medication name and opened the box. She slipped out the contents and opened out the leaflet. Thomas kept one eye on her as he took the tablet and gulped down a mouthful of water. The thin paper crackled in her fingers as her eyes scanned the page, front and back.

"Epilepsy, neuropathic pain, generalised anxiety disorder…" she read. "Are you anxious?"

Thomas shook his head.

"Epileptic?" Another shake. She kept on reading. "Peripheral and central pain…long-lasting pain." She slowly folded the paper and slipped it back into its box, along with the blister pack. Jen glanced at Pete then back at the old man in bed. Thomas stared back at her, unwavering, with the expression of a twelve-year-old caught cheating. An uneasy glint gave away his nerves.

"Have you told her," asked Jen softly.

Thomas paled but his eyes never left hers. Jen shook the second pack. "They don't give you these for nothing. You don't get these for flu or achy days…"

She remained focussed on Thomas, ignoring the uncomfortable standoff, until his pallid eyes glazed with unshed tears. She broke eye contact and fought back her own as he murmured almost inaudibly. "You won't tell her?"

Jen bit the inside of her lip and her mouth formed a thin line. Pete spoke for her. "Won't tell her what?"

"She thinks they're just to pep me up, keep me on my toes…" Thomas indicated the tablets. "And they work, most of the time. Today is just a bad day, tomorrow I'll be back to myself."

Jen couldn't trust herself to speak.

"Chicken soup," mumbled Thomas. "She thinks chicken soup will make me better, and it will. I'll be as right as rain tomorrow, you'll see."

Jen sank onto the bed. She took Thomas's hand. "How long?" She looked into the old man's eyes. "How long?"

Joan's footsteps on the stairs forced the conversation to close, but not before old Thomas looked Jen in the eye and whispered. "Not long, not long if this room full of angels is anything to go by…"

THIRTY-FIVE
BLUE

Freya's angels moved with her, but it was only ever Thomas who sensed them. The frisson between Freya's parents was electric and it left no room for anything else.

"Joe…" Rachel's voice was hesitant, nervous even. "We need to go to the beach."

Freya's father gazed at the lilac card in his hand. His eyes taking in his daughter's hand, reading the words she had written. He ran his thumb over the chocolate smear.

"We need to build a sandcastle," she said softly, "a good one."

"And paddle in the sea." He traced the words with his finger.

"And Joe…"

He heard her voice waver and he looked up. She didn't meet his eyes.

"Joe…can you wear your blue t-shirt?"

She didn't need to look at him to feel the energy in the room, but she did and this time she met his glistening eyes. He nodded and she smiled.

THIRTY-SIX
IMPOSSIBLE

Pete wandered down the passage beside the house. He was surprised that Thomas hadn't appeared as soon as he'd pulled up. Joan had accompanied Jen and Mrs French to the drapery store, to try out colours for the wedding, and at a loose end Pete had found himself outside the Hillman's home.

No one had answered the door and Pete's concern had grown, so he strolled down the passage. His apprehension lessened as singing drifted across the garden and into the corridor. Pete smiled and listened. The old man's voice rose, its pitch mounting and falling as he sang about quests and unreachable stars…

Pete grinned and ducked under a climbing rose. He moved into the back garden and scanned it for Thomas. The old man's voice wavered and mumbled and it took a moment for Pete to locate him amongst the tall, purple verbena bonariensis. Thomas was bent over a rose bush with his back to the house. Pete stopped and waited, and as Thomas straightened his voice got louder. The lyrics told of a heart, true to its dreams, at peace with itself and shivers shot down Pete's spine as he watched the old man, tall and erect, not a sign of the pain-ridden man from a month ago. Pete raised his hand to wave, and opened his mouth to call out, but he noticed the white wires twining down across Thomas's chest, and smiled at the earphones stuck in his ears. Old Thomas sang on, his voice strengthening with every word. Words that echoed Thomas's own heart and his desires, and strivings to reach that last distant dream…

His voice rose to a crescendo *"…the un-reach-able…"* and his voice broke, and Pete struggled to hold back the tears that pricked his eyes.

Pete couldn't speak. Then in one reckless moment of abandon he called out, loud and clear. "Thomas, Thomas!"

Above the music Thomas heard Pete call and he spun round. He pulled the earphones out and waved the wires. "Pete!" he called back, "This thingamabob thing actually works!" Thomas reached into his pocket and pulled out a tiny MP3, he screwed up his face. "How do I stop it then?"

"Thomas!" Pete's heart thumped like a battering ram against his ribcage. "Thomas."

"I'm coming, I'm coming," replied Thomas his face red and bright. Thomas dropped the pruning shears on the ground and hurried down his garden, intrigued by the urgency in Pete's voice. "What's up? Are the girls' alright?"

"They're fine," interrupted Pete, he took a deep breath; he couldn't believe he was about to do this. "Thomas…"

"Stop wasting my name and spit it out young man."

"I, you…"

Thomas grinned. "Cat got your tongue?"

"The bike…"

Thomas started off down the passage. "What's with the bike?"

"Thomas, do you have a helmet?"

Thomas stopped dead. "A what?" he asked without turning.

"A helmet, or would Jen's fit do you think?"

"Jen's would look better," offered Thomas, "if I had to wear one. I've got an old jacket though, it's a good one."

"Get the jacket."

Thomas still didn't turn back, but moved quickly into the house and returned a few minutes later with a big blouson, black bike jacket. "It's not fashionable, but it's good leather and when did I ever care about fashion?" Pete took it and held it out for the old man. Thomas put his arm in one side and Pete helped with the other. Thomas zipped it up.

Pete clumped up the passage. Thomas stayed rooted to the spot. "I haven't got boots," he said.

Pete called back. "Doesn't matter, your garden shoes are strong enough."

Thomas followed, his heart speeding up, threatening to match the drum that beat within Pete's own chest.

At the bike, Pete unattached Jen's helmet and handed it to Thomas. For a split second Thomas hesitated, and the two men stared at each other, Pete's green eyes meeting Thomas's piercing brown ones. "It's okay, you're not riding on your own, you're going on the back."

"I don't know if I can," admitted Thomas, his legs suddenly turning to jelly. He reached out for the helmet, his hands trembling, and placed it upon his head. Pete tightened the chinstrap and clipped it, and lifted the visor. "I don't know if I can…" Thomas shook his head as Pete handed him Jen's gloves.

"Do you want to?" asked Pete.

Thomas nodded, his head wobbling with the weight of the helmet. "More than anything, more than anything in the world…"

And that's where Freya jumped in.

Pete got on the bike and looked round at Thomas. He nodded. Thomas placed his hands on Pete's waist and the bike, and began to lift his leg. He quivered and painful tears welled in his eyes, but suddenly he felt light and his leg straddled the bike with ease, as Freya mirrored his every move. He blinked the tears away and lowered the visor. Even clothed in thick gloves, his hands suddenly felt supple and strong and Thomas clung to Pete's waist.

The motorbike coughed and purred into action and Thomas grinned. Pete flipped down his visor and glanced over his shoulder and gently pulled away from the curb.

Thomas clung tightly to Pete's leather jacket, and behind him, Freya wrapped her arms around Thomas, her head resting against his back.

Freya could feel the emotions surging through old Thomas, and a bond was formed as she unknowingly strengthened him.

Pete rode carefully, steadily, gently, fully aware of the old, fragile man riding pillion. Then as they stopped at traffic lights he felt Thomas let go with one hand and heard him lift the visor. He waited; feeling guilt rise, fully expecting Thomas to ask to be taken home, but the words surprised him and made him smile. "Go on, don't mind me…" Thomas broke into song, *"This is my quest… don't make it unreachable!"*

He clamped his visor back down and gripped Pete tightly again, and Pete revved the engine. He heard Thomas's muffled whoop of joy and twisted the throttle. The bike leapt away as the lights changed and Pete surged down the road, his original plan of gently wandering the local neighbourhood, quashed by the old man's desire.

Moments later they were speeding down the bypass, towards the back roads and Thomas was howling with delight!

They rode, with hearts on fire. The bike moving to Pete's every command, and Thomas, enjoying every moment. Life flowing through the old man's veins, elation making him light-headed with every curve and weave of the road.

Thomas was a young man again, soaring through the sky, flying like a bird, memories coursing through his old body…recollections filling every pore and thrills spilling over his soul. Thomas couldn't remember ever feeling this good!

Thomas knew that he had, at last, achieved his dream, the one that had kept him alive.

THIRTY-SEVEN
UNREACHABLE

The solemn assembly sat watching Freya pull petals off a white rose. "He's ready," she said.

"You knew that ages ago," pointed out Sophie.

"But I didn't know what to do about it then," replied Freya.

"He got the motorbike ride…and his wife didn't kill him!" Keira grinned.

"Pete didn't kill him!" said Abu.

Freya shot him a glare. "I was there, Uncle Pete did what he had to!" Freya cast her mind back.

Joan *had* threatened to kill Thomas, she'd threatened to walk out, and Jen had, likewise threatened to cancel the wedding… The two women had arrived home to an empty house, pruning shears dumped among the roses, music player, trailing its headphones still playing songs, left halfway down the side passage and Thomas's olive green cardigan hung on the gatepost. They had searched the house, fear growing in the pits of their bellies, until they had rushed outside at the sound of a droning motorbike.

Joan had stopped dead at the sight of her husband dressed in an ancient leather jacket and Jen's helmet. Jen had just managed to sidestep her and stormed up the path to the gate. "What on earth do you think you are doing?" she demanded, her eyes alight with fire.

Thomas lifted his visor and giggled, a childish sound, and he patted Pete on the shoulder. "Sorry mate, she's all yours!" he laughed.

Pete glanced further and leaned back to Thomas. "Don't like the look of yours much either," he confided.

The men smirked and Pete mumbled. "Do you want to go again? Shall we?" He twisted the throttle, but Thomas shook his head. "Love to mate, but I think that would only add to the flames of fury…"

They laughed again and Thomas climbed off the bike. He bent over and dramatically kissed the seat then straightened and sighed. One last look at Pete and he stepped forward. Thomas struggled with the helmet, unable to unclasp the safety catch, and Jen unfolded her arms and reached out. She unclipped it and Thomas pulled the helmet off. He feigned a forlorn face and handed it to Jen.

"Well, at least you were wearing it," she said between thin lips.

"Thank you, my dear," Thomas tapped her on the shoulder and lifted his head to meet his wife's glare. "Off to face the music then." He turned back to Jen, placing his hand on her arm. "Don't be too hard on him…he had to do it,"

"You made him?" She looked surprised.

Thomas chuckled and shook his head. "I had to do it, it was my unreachable star."

"Your what?"

Thomas let go and moved away. Freya saw Jen turn her head and watch as he strolled nonchalantly towards his wife. He had a spring in his step and he looked years younger…

Freya studied Joan, the old woman was mad, furious even, but behind her anger was an unguarded look of gratitude, and sadness, and as Thomas approached her Freya knew that Joan knew.

◆◆◆◆◆

Up in her garden, sitting beneath the willow, Freya stared down and the river before them faded. A firm look appeared on her face. "*I'm* ready."

The small group of friends leaned forward and Keira chuckled as Freya tumbled out of heaven. "There she goes…"

"She's got to do what she has to do," said Alice.

◆◆◆◆◆

Thomas was frail. The summer sun was fading and Thomas along with it.

"I don't know what gave you those extra months, was it the bike?" Joan mused, stroking her husband's brow. "But it was worth it, whatever it was."

Thomas murmured. "It was."

"I always knew, you know." Joan took his hand. "Do you want to know when I first knew?"

His head barely moved.

"I'll tell you," she spoke softly. "It was at young Freya's funeral. There was something about you…about everyone that day, it was so awful, such a baby, so little and yet gone…but you, she just about broke your heart."

Joan felt tears slip down her cheek as her husband squeezed her hand.

"She loved you, Thomas, they all loved you, but the day she told you, you were her best Sunday school teacher, you were so proud," she paused, "It was in the chapel, as we sat waiting. Then the little ones sang, all the children, they sang and it was like each little one was an angel. Thomas, I knew then, I felt it, I felt your heart break…it broke and you squeezed my hand."

Thomas tried to speak, but couldn't.

"What is it, sweetheart?" she asked. "I knew about the pills…" She choked. "I knew…"

Thomas opened his eyes. "Here…"

"Who's here? I'm here, I'm always here…"

He repeated the word and Joan frowned. "I'll be here."

They sat silently, accompanied only by the soft strains of welsh baritone emanating from the CD player and Thomas tried again. "She's here…"

Freya nodded, moved to his side and whispered. "I'm here."

"You're here," he murmured.

Joan stroked the back of his aged hand. "I'm here sweetheart, of course I'm here."

Freya whispered again. "I'm ready, I'll wait for you."

"I'm ready…" Thomas's words fought to escape his dry mouth.

Joan faced him. "You're ready?" she whispered. "*I'm* not."

"I'm ready," he repeated.

"*I'm* not, Tom, I'm not, not yet…Oh Tom." Joan moved closer to her husband and rested her head beside his on the stack of pillows. She caressed his brow and knew that the time had come for goodbyes.

THIRTY-EIGHT
SANDCASTLE

The late September sun was hiding behind a cloud, but the building went on. Uncle Pete had laid the foundation and built up a huge mound of sand with help from Joe and some obstruction from Jasmine. Now Jasmine had given up on the sandcastle and was trailing her Mum and Jen collecting pebbles and shells.

Her pockets and her bucket were stuffed with black mussels, white and lilac striped pearly shells, broken pieces of razor shell and an assortment of others. Her knees were sandy and her shorts were wet, but she was happy.

Rachel wandered along the shore with Jen, enjoying the warmth of the late summer sea. They dragged their feet through the rippling waves and discussed Jen's upcoming wedding.

"Jasmine's dress looks so gorgeous on her, the colours go so well, what flowers did you decide on in the end?" asked Rachel.

I've decided on cream roses, ones with a hint of blush and lots of dark green foliage, lots of greenery, ferns and stuff. It's my hair you see," said Jen. "Jasmine's dress is just the right green to go with my auburn hair, it's too red to go for pastels or pink or even lilac, but green looks heavenly, so lots of emerald to offset the white dress and cream roses."

"Good choice, I really love the dress," replied Rachel.

"Mine or the bridesmaid's?"

"Both!" Rachel laughed. "Yours is beautiful, tailored just right for you, simple but so beautiful, and I love the sleeves!"

"I love the veil," Jen enthused and the conversation continued in the same vein, so much so that Jasmine tuned out and concentrated on collecting the right shells.

Back with Joe and Pete, Rachel announced, "We have paddled," and the two men spread their arms to encompass the growing castle. "We are building!"

The mound had been flattened on top and Joe was making sandcastles in the square bucket with turreted corners, which were placed on the corners of the mound. He sat back on his heels and surveyed the work while Pete continued digging a moat with his hands. "It's easier than using the spade!" he told them pointing at the discarded children's spade.

"I got shells," said Jasmine tipping out her bucket and emptying her pockets.

"Brilliant!" said Uncle Pete. "I love those!"

Jasmine beamed and plonked herself down beside him. Her father grabbed her bucket and filled it and placed the round bucketful in the centre of the castle. He then built up around it, smoothing the slanting sides and dumped another bucketful on top.

"There!" he exclaimed. "That's the castle built!"

"Just a minute," puffed Pete, clawing out more wet sand, "As quick as I get it out, it slips back in!"

"Leave it, it's fine like that," said Jen. "Do you want us to go and get water…for the moat?"

Joe nodded.

Jen picked up two buckets and held out her hand for Jasmine. "C'mon then Jaz let's go, leave the guys to it."

Jasmine grabbed her hand and hauled herself up then ran ahead down the beach. Jen blew Pete a kiss and chased after the little girl.

Joe sank down beside his wife, and took her hand. "Eeergh!" She dropped his wet, sandy hand and giggled. He kissed her instead. "That's better!" She laughed.

"Do you like it?" he asked.

Rachel gazed at the sandcastle and smiled. "Right, now for the decoration. Then I might like it!" she joked.

She picked up a stick and began tracing arched windows onto the sides.

"Be careful!" cried Pete, "Don't knock all the sand off!"

"I won't," said Rachel, drawing a door on the side.

She then began arranging shells, pushing them in on the walls and laying them on top.

"Careful, I said!" shouted Pete, grinning as clumps of 'wall' fell off the side.

Rachel giggled. "I'm being as careful as I can!"

"I remember the castles you made as a kid!" said Pete, "They all fell down too!"

"Thank you!" Rachel feigned annoyance and carried on decorating.

Joe stood up and wandered off and came back a few minutes later with a long stick and tiny square of discarded green netting. "A flag," he told them, winding the string around the stick. Rachel nodded and he plunged it into the centre of the castle. "There."

"No drawbridge then?" Rachel asked Pete as he sat back, giving up on making the moat any deeper.

"I don't think so," he replied. "Far too complicated!"

"For you, maybe," his sister joked.

"Definitely for you!" he retorted. "And look here comes the water…"

Rachel spun round to check the sea, but the tide was still a long way out. Wandering back up the beach came Jen and Jasmine, slopping water over the sides of their buckets.

"Are you ready with the camera?" Rachel asked her husband.

"Yes, but you take the picture." He handed her the camera.

She unclipped the lens cover and held the camera up. Jen waved and Rachel clicked. Jasmine ran and her bucket slopped even more. Rachel caught a picture of her daughter, and then Pete met Jasmine and took the bucket from her. He helped his niece pour the water into the moat and grinned at Jen as she emptied hers in too.

"Be quick with the picture!" he cried, "The water's draining away!"

Rachel clicked and captured the castle then she got down onto the sand and got a frame from ground level. "Get in the picture," she ordered. "Jaz first." She snapped Jasmine standing behind the castle with her hands clapping in delight. Then the boys and Jen joined Jasmine. Rachel peered at the camera and mentally framed the picture she wanted. She placed the camera on a big pebble and set the timer. She scrambled up and ran behind the castle. "Smile, say cheese!" she demanded and they all waited with happy expressions fixed in place.

Rachel checked the picture and grinned. "Brilliant, and one take! I *am* good!"

They sat and basked, not in the sun, which was still veiled by cloud, but in a good day's work. A little later Pete reached out and pulled on his t-shirt. "That's it," he said checking his watch, "C'mon Jen, we've got to go, get back to your Mum's."

Joe grinned. "Are you keeping her daughter out too late?" he asked.

Pete swiped at him with the back of his hand. "Ha, ha," he said with sarcasm. "No, we promised to go over the order of service with her, invitations and all that, she's got contacts, we can get a good deal."

Jen smiled. "It's her wedding gift to us, she's got some gorgeous stationary."

Rachel nodded. "Thanks for coming with us, it's been lovely today."

"Sorry about the sun though," said Pete, waving up at the grey sky.

"Not to worry," said Rachel. "It's my fault I left it so late, it still took me ages to get my head round all of her list. Today, I don't know why it's today, we didn't plan it, it's just right today…"

Pete nodded and tousled Jasmine's hair. "Bye then trouble."

"Bye, tubble you!" Jasmine laughed and reached up for a kiss and a sandy hug.

Jen hugged her too and they disappeared across the beach.

Jasmine busied herself with the bucket and spade and her own sandcastle, and Joe put his arm around Rachel.

"Why today?" murmured Rachel. "What makes today special?" She sighed.

"There doesn't have to be a reason." Joe tightened his arm around her, and she leaned into him, pressing her face into his blue t-shirt.

Rachel sighed again and Joe could feel his wife tremble. "Something's missing," she whispered.

As a tear slipped out of her eye, a big fat raindrop fell from above, leaving an indentation in the wet sand. Just a few fell and Rachel stared out at the ocean. "Where are you, Freya…where are you?"

THIRTY-NINE
BREATH

Rachel hugged her husband's arm to her and brushed her lips across his skin. She closed her eyes trying to block thoughts of her daughter, but the hairs along his forearm touching her lips suddenly evoked memories of soft baby hair, and she kissed his arm as if it had been Freya's newborn head.

Her mind whirled and her heart hiccupped and emotions overwhelmed her. Rachel fell forward onto her knees then climbed to her feet. She stared wildly at the gentle waves lapping at the shore and stumbled forward. Joe sensed the need in his wife and let her go, staying instead with his remaining daughter, his solace.

Rachel walked across the sand, ignoring the raindrops that joined the tears making tracks down her face.

Her feet moved swiftly over the sand, splashing through the sheen of water gilding the shore. The tide was far out and the beach almost void of people. The evening mist settled, casting a shroud over the distant coast.

Rachel kept walking, her eyes roaming the horizon. "Freya…" she called, and listened as the word floated away on the light breeze. "Freya," she whispered, letting her daughter's name roll from her lips.

Her long skirt wrapped around her legs as she walked, her heart hammered and her mind beheld her daughter, as memories swirled amid tears.

Late September's evening warmth enveloped her and the sun finally broke through the overcast sky. For the first time that day weak rays shone through the clouds and Rachel felt them tickle her bare arms. Goosebumps spread, sending a shiver throughout her body and she tingled.

The rain stopped, but moisture still hung heavy in the air and Freya's mother fell to her knees. Soft sand welcomed her and warm water seeped through her splayed fingers and across her hands after she dropped to all fours. She hung her head and allowed her tears to drop, unhindered, into the surrounding ocean's puddle. "Oh Freya, I need you, where are you?"

Freya knelt on the sand, her nose almost touching her mother's soft, mussed-up hair. "I'm here," she whispered, caught between heaven and earth by her mother's overwhelming pain.

Rachel's shoulders shook and her breaths came fast and choked as she tried to control the anguish that threatened to dominate, but nothing could contain her crushing grief and her silent tears became an audible lamentation. Her sorrow carried on a gust of wind that whipped her hair across her face and whisked her heartache out across the ocean.

Her daughter stood before her, fraught innocence and intense sadness etched into her shining face, but nothing made an impression.

"I'm here…I'm here!" Freya's voice rose in frustration. "See me, *please* see me!" But her pleas fell on deaf ears and her mother continued weeping.

Instead, Freya lingered at her mother's side, waiting, waiting for a lull, waiting for a sign to guide her. Freya wondered why she couldn't touch her mother, why she couldn't leave an impression, why she couldn't write in the sand and connect with her mother, Freya wondered why?

Rachel connected, but it was with wet sand, her skirt was soaked and her knees were sinking, and she had no choice but to stand. She wiped sandy hands on her sodden skirt and tucked stray hair behind her ear. Rachel sighed and took a deep breath, and finally, was quiet.

She stared blindly out across the water, and let her arms hang limply at her side. Then she began to walk steadily and resolutely towards the sea.

Freya ran alongside her, tugging at her skirt, fretting and fussing, but to no gain, Rachel just kept walking.

Freya tried to leave, but unseen cords held her, checking her and Freya was lost…she had no idea what to do. She was ready, but her mother's anguish held her, and nothing could change until Freya had forged a bond, a heavenly bond with her mother.

But time was running out. Old Thomas had a matter of moments and Freya had a promise to keep.

Little lights flit about in the sky above them, but only Freya could see them, and then Alice dipped and was walking beside Freya with Rachel's footprints gathered momentum behind them. Alice tapped her wrist and despite it being void of a wristwatch, Freya understood. Freya shrugged and shook her head. "I don't know what to do…I can't leave her like this."

Alice smiled. "There's only one thing you can do…and it's the perfect time."

Freya frowned but before she had a chance to speak Alice had vanished, disappearing into the pale rays that shone through the grey clouds. Then Freya knew exactly what she had to do.

Excitement effervesced and Freya's joy almost bubbled over in anticipation as she ran ahead and leapt up into the sky. Freya danced becoming one with the elements, and made the most of the pale sun, the raindrops still hanging in the air and the backdrop of the ocean.

First she conjured scarlet, as vivid as remembrance poppies, sunset orange to offset the red and sunflower yellow came next. Then green, like her willow, and blue…the exact shade of daddy's t-shirt, and then she drew on the colour of deepening night to form indigo and finished with Purple Ted's violet hue.

Then she waited.

As the rainbow appeared Rachel slowed, her mouth dropped open and her eyes stared in wonder. Her heart pounded and her spine prickled, and fresh tears misted her eyes.

"Oh, Freya…your rainbow!" she whispered. "Freya! Freya!" Her voice rose. "Freya, number ten! Freya it's your rainbow!"

Rachel's heart spilled over and she roughly wiped her tears away. She broke into a run and hurried forward then stopped and laughed, her peal of laughter ringing in the air. "Your rainbow!" she cried. "Freya's rainbow!"

Freya wiped away her own tears and stood waiting beneath the arc, watching her mother.

Exaltation filled Rachel's soul as she stood gazing in awe at the divine phenomenon. She blinked and followed the arc with her eyes taking in every colour. It faded into the ocean at the far end, and Rachel cast her eyes across its bow. The rainbow hovered, beginning some feet above the sand a little way ahead of her, or so it seemed. Again, she skipped forward and ran towards it, but with every step it moved further away, yet remained the same…

Freya's mother stopped again and placed her hands on her knees, bending forward. She laughed again, allowing the endorphins to fizz through her, making her dizzy. The rainbow reflected across the wet sand and as Rachel looked up she thought about her daughter.

Freya watched with love bursting from every pore, knowing that her mother had found her answer, feeling the restraints ping away, and a celestial call seeped through her body beckoning her home.

Her eyes searched the beach and set upon her little sister and her father. Both together, Jasmine sitting astride her father's knee, and both staring with delight at the most beautiful rainbow they had ever seen, a rainbow that hung in the sky with such glory and clarity that neither could take their eyes off of it.

Jasmine turned to her dad and grabbed his t-shirt. "You blue top Daddy, like that rainbow, and green like mine t-shirt."

"And purple like Freya's teddy bear." Daddy smiled. "And beautiful like Freya," he murmured.

Freya turned back to her mother, who still stood awestruck. "Goodbye," she said softly, "Goodbye." Freya stood at the foot of the rainbow and turned her face heavenward. "I'm ready…I'm ready!"

Then the heavens truly opened. Raindrops fell from the sky, huge, round drops that exploded as they hit the sand, and splashed at Rachel's feet. Rachel grinned and listened as the pitter-patter around her got louder and she lifted her head to the rain, letting it drench her face, and she swept back her hair and spread out her arms, and called. "Freya, I'm here…under your rainbow!" Then Rachel stared through the curtain of rain and her heart skipped and she trembled and her breath caught in her throat, and nothing could move her, and she stared in disbelief at the girl who stood beneath the rainbow.

Rachel could not blink, or breathe, or stir, as she beheld a young woman, a girl with long, brown hair and green eyes, a girl who was so beautiful that Rachel's heart stood still. A girl who could be no one but her daughter…

Rachel blinked and Freya moved on, just a breath away.

EPILOGUE
WOKEN SOUL

It was the willow that Freya was drawn to. She wandered through her bluebells, moving instinctively. As she left the shade of her old gnarled woodland, she was conscious of the souls she was leaving behind, but their joy infused her, and she drifted on.

Diamond-encrusted grass, heavy with dew, bathed her feet as she walked, and bluebells sprang up through the greensward with every step, creating a carpet of blue trailing behind her.

Freya, charged with heady invigoration, sensed the change within and knew she was no longer an awkward seven-year-old. Her long legs carried her tall and strong, and feminine grace abounded. Her girly dress, once decorated with stars and ribbons had lengthened, and fit like a gossamer glove. Its lilac hue shimmered then faded into the purest white and Freya's hair glistened and hung about her shoulders, framing the face of a beautiful young woman.

The sky above was azure and gold and familiarity seeped through Freya's veins. Light immersed the landscape growing stronger all the time and Freya danced towards her willow's trembling boughs. Its feathery leaves, bleached by the surrounding brilliance, tickled Freya and she giggled then paused, almost bursting with excitement.

"Are you ready?" An ethereal, but melodious and gentle voice drifted through the light and a surge of energy suffused Freya.

"I made rainbows..." she replied.

The light brightened as if in answer and a play of light beckoned her. Freya hurried on as the willow's boughs parted and her soul awoke. Every sense in her body was heightened and exquisite. "I'm ready," she affirmed and was immediately swallowed up into the most brilliant radiance, and Freya felt as though she were one with every living soul. Then the brilliance faded and Freya found herself alone wandering through a misty meadow. She glanced around, her gown wafting in the cool breeze. She twirled several times, enjoying the sensation of harmony, and then a voice broke her reverie.

"Freya..."

She turned to see a man with piercing blue eyes and tawny brown hair, standing to her rear. He laughed and his laugh made her feel warm inside.

"Am I your assignment?" she asked with a smile.

"Not this time," he replied pushing his floppy hair out of his eyes.

Jake took her hand and she perceived his soul.

"I'm ready," she told him.

He smiled.

Freya's eyes were suddenly alert. "Thomas!" she exclaimed.

"Let's go." Jake nodded. "You have a promise to keep."

And with that they were gone...just a breath away.

The End

ABOUT THE AUTHOR

Born and raised in vibrant Brighton, England, Lisa's lyrical writing is emotional and imaginative. She concentrates on description and colour, and hopes her readers will easily visualise the narrative. Her first book *Beneath the Rainbow* is available on Amazon in both print and as an ebook for the Kindle.

A wife and mother, Lisa draws inspiration from family life, faith, memory and imagination. After having her first of three children, Lisa has lived in Carmarthen, West Wales, another town rich in legend and lore.

Lisa loves family time, walking the family's excitable German Shepherd, beaches, scrap-booking, photography, art and last, but not least, writing…she says, "There is nothing better than escaping and immersing yourself in a good story!"

Made in the USA
Charleston, SC
31 January 2014